THE STORY
OF THE OTHER
WISE MAN

and

OTHER CHRISTMAS
STORIES BY

HENRY VAN DYKE

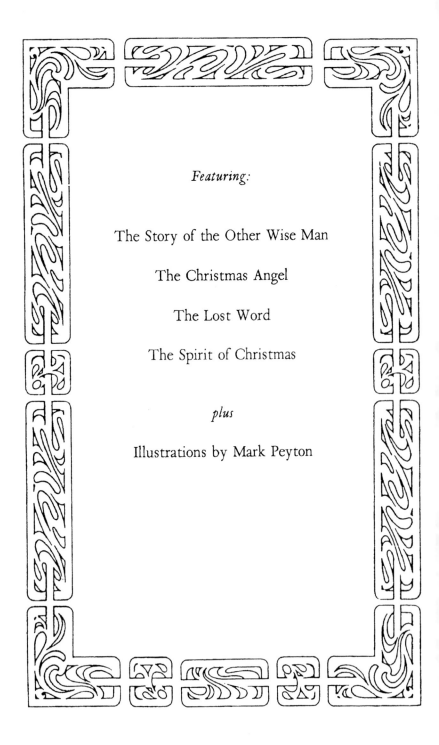

Featuring:

The Story of the Other Wise Man

The Christmas Angel

The Lost Word

The Spirit of Christmas

plus

Illustrations by Mark Peyton

THE STORY
OF THE OTHER
WISE MAN

and Other
Christmas Stories

BY HENRY VAN DYKE

ENTHEA PRESS
Columbus, Ohio

THE STORY OF THE OTHER WISE MAN

Artwork by Mark Peyton.

E-mail: www.lightariel.com

TABLE OF CONTENTS

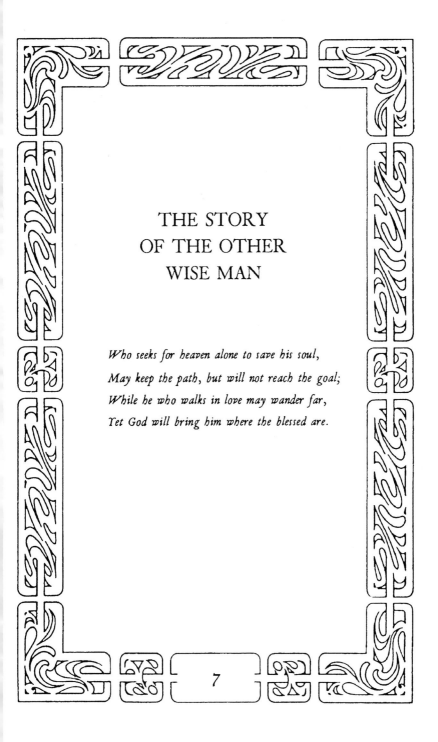

THE STORY
OF THE OTHER
WISE MAN

Who seeks for heaven alone to save his soul,
May keep the path, but will not reach the goal;
While he who walks in love may wander far,
Yet God will bring him where the blessed are.

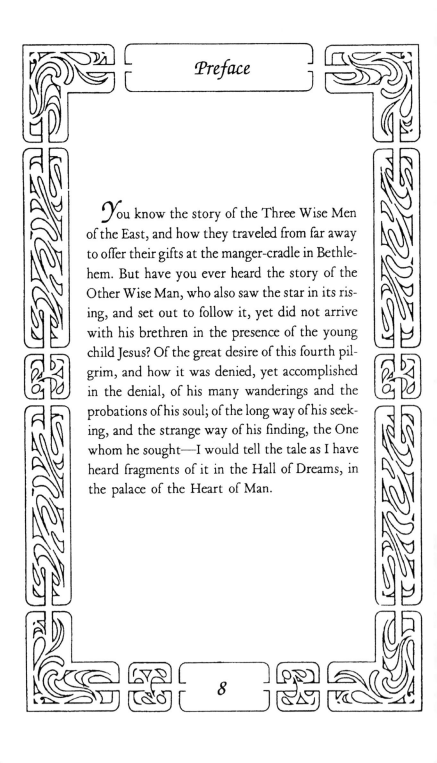

Preface

You know the story of the Three Wise Men of the East, and how they traveled from far away to offer their gifts at the manger-cradle in Bethlehem. But have you ever heard the story of the Other Wise Man, who also saw the star in its rising, and set out to follow it, yet did not arrive with his brethren in the presence of the young child Jesus? Of the great desire of this fourth pilgrim, and how it was denied, yet accomplished in the denial, of his many wanderings and the probations of his soul; of the long way of his seeking, and the strange way of his finding, the One whom he sought—I would tell the tale as I have heard fragments of it in the Hall of Dreams, in the palace of the Heart of Man.

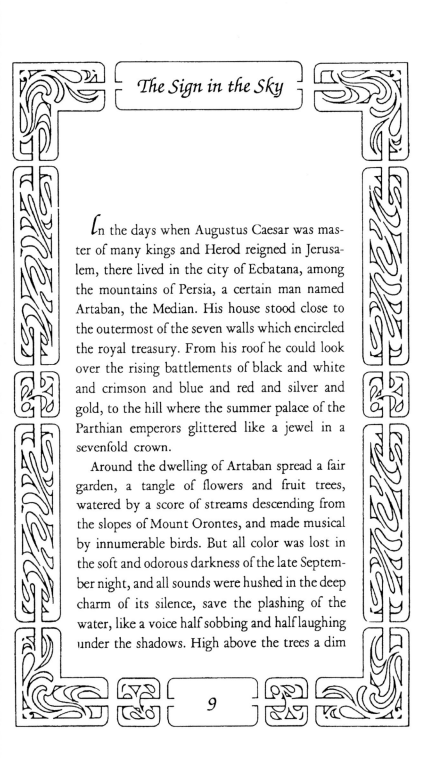

The Sign in the Sky

*I*n the days when Augustus Caesar was master of many kings and Herod reigned in Jerusalem, there lived in the city of Ecbatana, among the mountains of Persia, a certain man named Artaban, the Median. His house stood close to the outermost of the seven walls which encircled the royal treasury. From his roof he could look over the rising battlements of black and white and crimson and blue and red and silver and gold, to the hill where the summer palace of the Parthian emperors glittered like a jewel in a sevenfold crown.

Around the dwelling of Artaban spread a fair garden, a tangle of flowers and fruit trees, watered by a score of streams descending from the slopes of Mount Orontes, and made musical by innumerable birds. But all color was lost in the soft and odorous darkness of the late September night, and all sounds were hushed in the deep charm of its silence, save the plashing of the water, like a voice half sobbing and half laughing under the shadows. High above the trees a dim glow of light shone through the curtained arches of the upper chamber, where the master of the house was holding council with his friends.

He stood by the doorway to greet his guests—a tall, dark man of about forty years, with brilliant eyes set near together under his broad brow, and firm lines graven around his fine, thin lips; the brow of a dreamer and the mouth of a soldier, a man of sensitive feeling but inflexible will—one of those who, in whatever age they may live, are born for inward conflict and life of quest.

His robe was of pure white wool, thrown over a tunic of silk; and a white pointed cap, with long lapels at the sides, rested on his flowing black hair. It was the dress of the ancient priesthood of the Magi, called the fire-worshipers.

"Welcome!" he said, in his low, pleasant voice, as one after another entered the room— "welcome, Abdus; peace be with you, Rhodaspes and Tigranes, and with you my father, Abgarus. You are all welcome, and this house grows bright with the joy of your presence."

There were nine of the men, differing widely in age, but alike in the richness of their dress of many-colored silks, and in the massive golden collars around their necks, marking them as

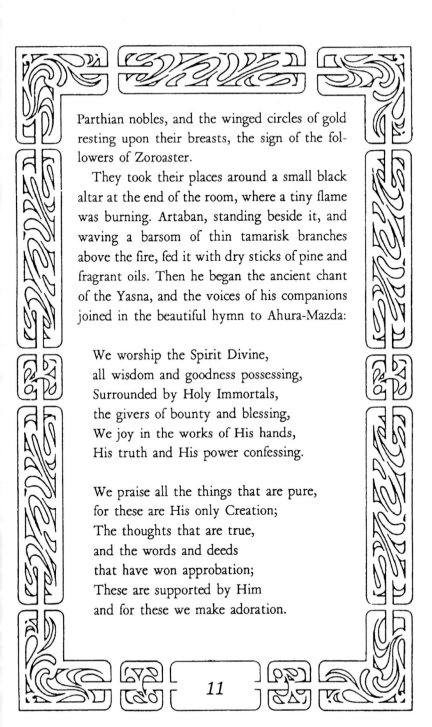

Parthian nobles, and the winged circles of gold resting upon their breasts, the sign of the followers of Zoroaster.

They took their places around a small black altar at the end of the room, where a tiny flame was burning. Artaban, standing beside it, and waving a barsom of thin tamarisk branches above the fire, fed it with dry sticks of pine and fragrant oils. Then he began the ancient chant of the Yasna, and the voices of his companions joined in the beautiful hymn to Ahura-Mazda:

We worship the Spirit Divine,
all wisdom and goodness possessing,
Surrounded by Holy Immortals,
the givers of bounty and blessing,
We joy in the works of His hands,
His truth and His power confessing.

We praise all the things that are pure,
for these are His only Creation;
The thoughts that are true,
and the words and deeds
that have won approbation;
These are supported by Him
and for these we make adoration.

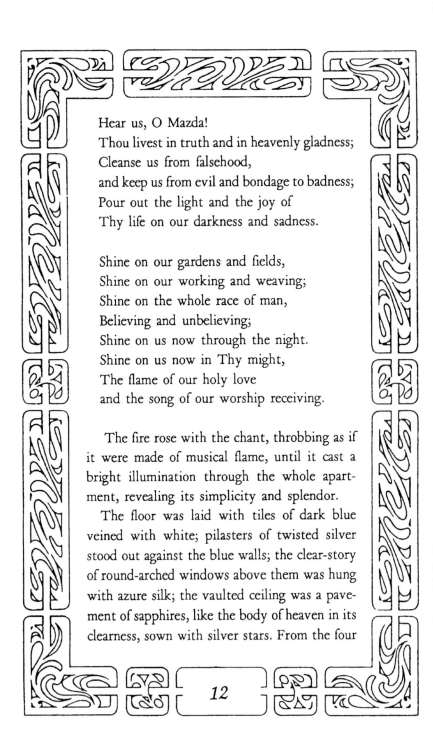

Hear us, O Mazda!
Thou livest in truth and in heavenly gladness;
Cleanse us from falsehood,
and keep us from evil and bondage to badness;
Pour out the light and the joy of
Thy life on our darkness and sadness.

Shine on our gardens and fields,
Shine on our working and weaving;
Shine on the whole race of man,
Believing and unbelieving;
Shine on us now through the night.
Shine on us now in Thy might,
The flame of our holy love
and the song of our worship receiving.

The fire rose with the chant, throbbing as if
it were made of musical flame, until it cast a
bright illumination through the whole apart-
ment, revealing its simplicity and splendor.

The floor was laid with tiles of dark blue
veined with white; pilasters of twisted silver
stood out against the blue walls; the clear-story
of round-arched windows above them was hung
with azure silk; the vaulted ceiling was a pave-
ment of sapphires, like the body of heaven in its
clearness, sown with silver stars. From the four

corners of the roof hung four golden magic-wheels, called the tongues of the gods. At the eastern end, behind the altar, there were two dark-red pillars of porphyry; above them a lintel of the same stone, on which was carved the figure of a winged archer, with his arrow set to the string and his bow drawn.

The doorway between the pillars, which opened upon the terrace of the roof, was covered with a heavy curtain of the color of a ripe pomegranate, embroidered with innumerable golden rays shooting upward from the floor. In effect the room was like a quiet, starry night, all azure and silver, flushed in the east with rosy promise of the dawn. It was, as the house of a man should be, an expression of the character and spirit of the master.

He turned to his friends when the song was ended, and invited them to be seated on the divan at the western end of the room.

"You have come tonight," said he, looking around the circle, "at my call, as the faithful scholars of Zoroaster, to renew your worship and rekindle your faith in the God of Purity, even as this fire has been rekindled on the altar. We worship not the fire, but Him of whom it is the chosen symbol, because it is the purest of all

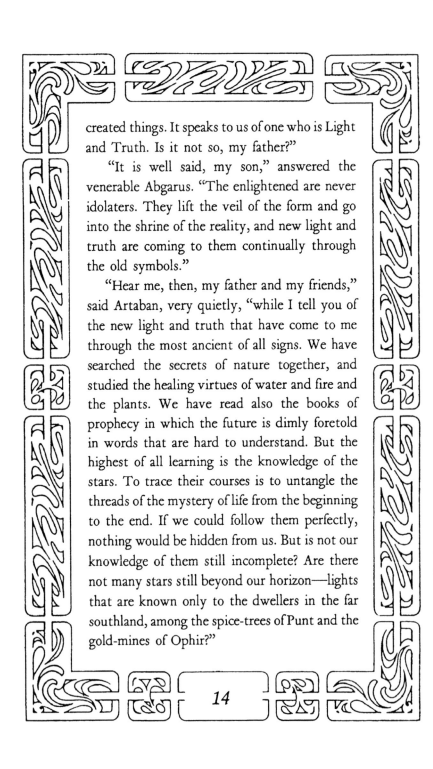

created things. It speaks to us of one who is Light and Truth. Is it not so, my father?"

"It is well said, my son," answered the venerable Abgarus. "The enlightened are never idolaters. They lift the veil of the form and go into the shrine of the reality, and new light and truth are coming to them continually through the old symbols."

"Hear me, then, my father and my friends," said Artaban, very quietly, "while I tell you of the new light and truth that have come to me through the most ancient of all signs. We have searched the secrets of nature together, and studied the healing virtues of water and fire and the plants. We have read also the books of prophecy in which the future is dimly foretold in words that are hard to understand. But the highest of all learning is the knowledge of the stars. To trace their courses is to untangle the threads of the mystery of life from the beginning to the end. If we could follow them perfectly, nothing would be hidden from us. But is not our knowledge of them still incomplete? Are there not many stars still beyond our horizon—lights that are known only to the dwellers in the far southland, among the spice-trees of Punt and the gold-mines of Ophir?"

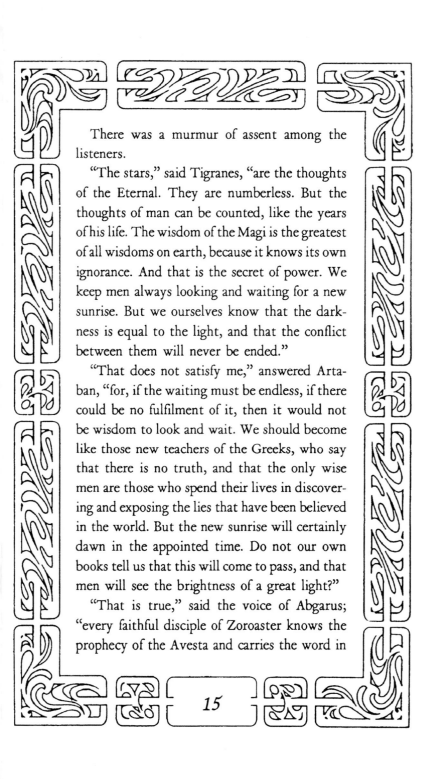

There was a murmur of assent among the listeners.

"The stars," said Tigranes, "are the thoughts of the Eternal. They are numberless. But the thoughts of man can be counted, like the years of his life. The wisdom of the Magi is the greatest of all wisdoms on earth, because it knows its own ignorance. And that is the secret of power. We keep men always looking and waiting for a new sunrise. But we ourselves know that the darkness is equal to the light, and that the conflict between them will never be ended."

"That does not satisfy me," answered Artaban, "for, if the waiting must be endless, if there could be no fulfilment of it, then it would not be wisdom to look and wait. We should become like those new teachers of the Greeks, who say that there is no truth, and that the only wise men are those who spend their lives in discovering and exposing the lies that have been believed in the world. But the new sunrise will certainly dawn in the appointed time. Do not our own books tell us that this will come to pass, and that men will see the brightness of a great light?"

"That is true," said the voice of Abgarus; "every faithful disciple of Zoroaster knows the prophecy of the Avesta and carries the word in

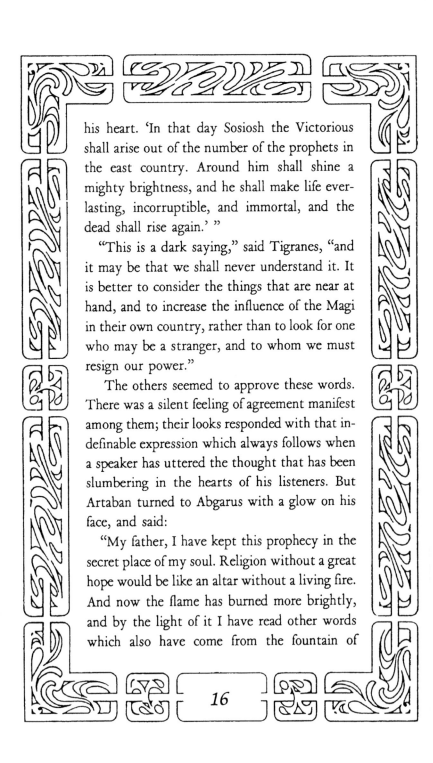

his heart. 'In that day Sosiosh the Victorious shall arise out of the number of the prophets in the east country. Around him shall shine a mighty brightness, and he shall make life everlasting, incorruptible, and immortal, and the dead shall rise again.' "

"This is a dark saying," said Tigranes, "and it may be that we shall never understand it. It is better to consider the things that are near at hand, and to increase the influence of the Magi in their own country, rather than to look for one who may be a stranger, and to whom we must resign our power."

The others seemed to approve these words. There was a silent feeling of agreement manifest among them; their looks responded with that indefinable expression which always follows when a speaker has uttered the thought that has been slumbering in the hearts of his listeners. But Artaban turned to Abgarus with a glow on his face, and said:

"My father, I have kept this prophecy in the secret place of my soul. Religion without a great hope would be like an altar without a living fire. And now the flame has burned more brightly, and by the light of it I have read other words which also have come from the fountain of

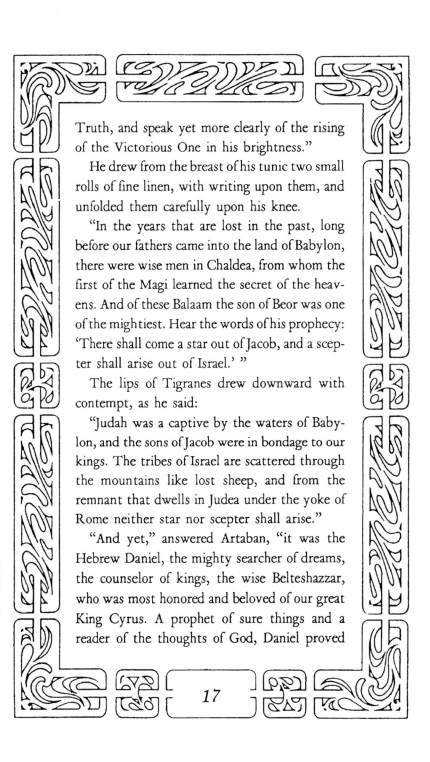

Truth, and speak yet more clearly of the rising of the Victorious One in his brightness."

He drew from the breast of his tunic two small rolls of fine linen, with writing upon them, and unfolded them carefully upon his knee.

"In the years that are lost in the past, long before our fathers came into the land of Babylon, there were wise men in Chaldea, from whom the first of the Magi learned the secret of the heavens. And of these Balaam the son of Beor was one of the mightiest. Hear the words of his prophecy: 'There shall come a star out of Jacob, and a scepter shall arise out of Israel.' "

The lips of Tigranes drew downward with contempt, as he said:

"Judah was a captive by the waters of Babylon, and the sons of Jacob were in bondage to our kings. The tribes of Israel are scattered through the mountains like lost sheep, and from the remnant that dwells in Judea under the yoke of Rome neither star nor scepter shall arise."

"And yet," answered Artaban, "it was the Hebrew Daniel, the mighty searcher of dreams, the counselor of kings, the wise Belteshazzar, who was most honored and beloved of our great King Cyrus. A prophet of sure things and a reader of the thoughts of God, Daniel proved

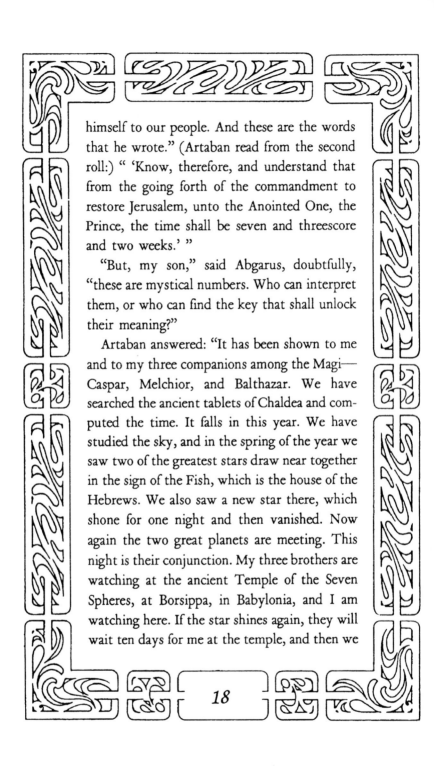

himself to our people. And these are the words that he wrote." (Artaban read from the second roll:) " 'Know, therefore, and understand that from the going forth of the commandment to restore Jerusalem, unto the Anointed One, the Prince, the time shall be seven and threescore and two weeks.' "

"But, my son," said Abgarus, doubtfully, "these are mystical numbers. Who can interpret them, or who can find the key that shall unlock their meaning?"

Artaban answered: "It has been shown to me and to my three companions among the Magi—Caspar, Melchior, and Balthazar. We have searched the ancient tablets of Chaldea and computed the time. It falls in this year. We have studied the sky, and in the spring of the year we saw two of the greatest stars draw near together in the sign of the Fish, which is the house of the Hebrews. We also saw a new star there, which shone for one night and then vanished. Now again the two great planets are meeting. This night is their conjunction. My three brothers are watching at the ancient Temple of the Seven Spheres, at Borsippa, in Babylonia, and I am watching here. If the star shines again, they will wait ten days for me at the temple, and then we will set out together for Jerusalem, to see and worship the promised one who shall be born King of Israel. I believe the sign will come. I have made ready for the journey. I have sold my house and my possessions, and bought these three jewels—a sapphire, a ruby, and a pearl—to carry them as tribute to the King. And I ask you to go with me on the pilgrimage, that we may have joy together in finding the Prince who is worthy to be served."

While he was speaking he thrust his hand into the inmost fold of his girdle and drew out three great gems—one blue as a fragment of the night sky, one redder than a ray of sunrise, and one as pure as the peak of a snow mountain at twilight—and laid them on the outspread linen scrolls before him.

But his friends looked on with strange and alien eyes. A veil of doubt and mistrust came over their faces, like a fog creeping up from the marshes to hide the hills. They glanced at each other with looks of wonder and pity, as those who have listened to incredible sayings, the story of a wild vision, or the proposal of an impossible enterprise.

At last Tigranes said: "Artaban, this is a vain dream. It comes from too much looking upon the

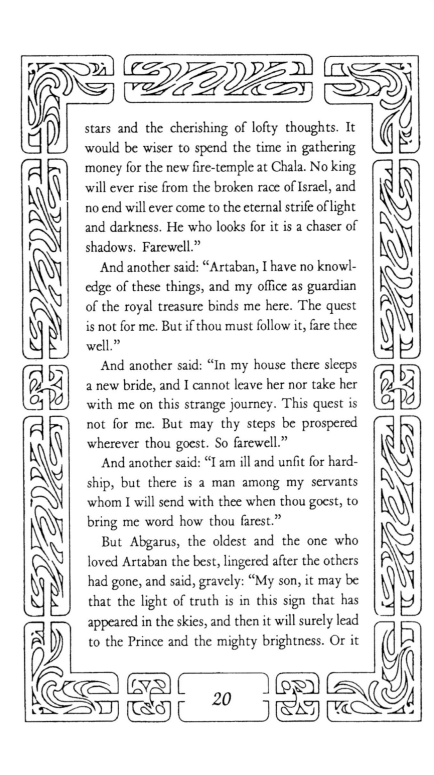

stars and the cherishing of lofty thoughts. It would be wiser to spend the time in gathering money for the new fire-temple at Chala. No king will ever rise from the broken race of Israel, and no end will ever come to the eternal strife of light and darkness. He who looks for it is a chaser of shadows. Farewell."

And another said: "Artaban, I have no knowledge of these things, and my office as guardian of the royal treasure binds me here. The quest is not for me. But if thou must follow it, fare thee well."

And another said: "In my house there sleeps a new bride, and I cannot leave her nor take her with me on this strange journey. This quest is not for me. But may thy steps be prospered wherever thou goest. So farewell."

And another said: "I am ill and unfit for hardship, but there is a man among my servants whom I will send with thee when thou goest, to bring me word how thou farest."

But Abgarus, the oldest and the one who loved Artaban the best, lingered after the others had gone, and said, gravely: "My son, it may be that the light of truth is in this sign that has appeared in the skies, and then it will surely lead to the Prince and the mighty brightness. Or it

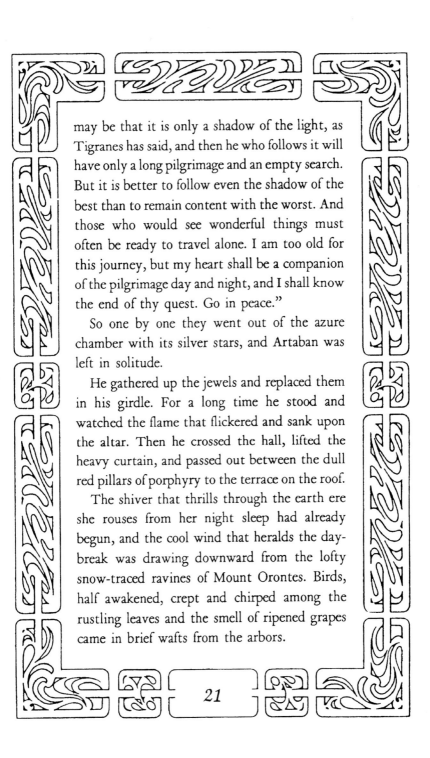

may be that it is only a shadow of the light, as Tigranes has said, and then he who follows it will have only a long pilgrimage and an empty search. But it is better to follow even the shadow of the best than to remain content with the worst. And those who would see wonderful things must often be ready to travel alone. I am too old for this journey, but my heart shall be a companion of the pilgrimage day and night, and I shall know the end of thy quest. Go in peace."

So one by one they went out of the azure chamber with its silver stars, and Artaban was left in solitude.

He gathered up the jewels and replaced them in his girdle. For a long time he stood and watched the flame that flickered and sank upon the altar. Then he crossed the hall, lifted the heavy curtain, and passed out between the dull red pillars of porphyry to the terrace on the roof.

The shiver that thrills through the earth ere she rouses from her night sleep had already begun, and the cool wind that heralds the day-break was drawing downward from the lofty snow-traced ravines of Mount Orontes. Birds, half awakened, crept and chirped among the rustling leaves and the smell of ripened grapes came in brief wafts from the arbors.

Far over the eastern plain a white mist stretched like a lake. But where the distant peak of Zagros serrated the western horizon the sky was clear. Jupiter and Saturn rolled together like drops of lambent flame about to blend in one.

As Artaban watched them, behold! an azure spark was born out of the darkness beneath, rounding itself with purple splendors to a crimson sphere, and spiring upward through rays of saffron and orange into a point of white radiance. Tiny and infinitely remote, yet perfect in every part, it pulsated in the enormous vault as if the three jewels in the Magian's breast had mingled and been transformed into a living heart of light.

He bowed his head. He covered his brow with his hands.

"It is the sign," he said. "The King is coming, and I will go to meet him."

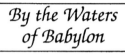

*A*ll night long Vasda, the swiftest of Artaban's horses, had been waiting, saddled and brid-
led, in her stall, pawing the ground impatiently
and shaking her bit as if she shared the eagerness
of her master's purpose, though she knew not its
meaning.

Before the birds had fully roused to their
strong, high, joyful chant of morning song, before the white mist had begun to lift lazily from
the plain, the Other Wise Man was in the saddle,
riding swiftly along the high road, which skirted
the base of Mount Orontes, westward.

How close, how intimate is the comradeship
between a man and his favorite horse on a long
journey. It is a silent, comprehensive friendship,
an intercourse beyond the need of words.

They drink at the same wayside spring, and
sleep under the same guardian stars. They are
conscious together of the subduing spell of nightfall and the quickening joy of daybreak. The
master shares his evening meal with his hungry
companion, and feels the soft, moist lips caress-
ing the palm of his hand as they close over the

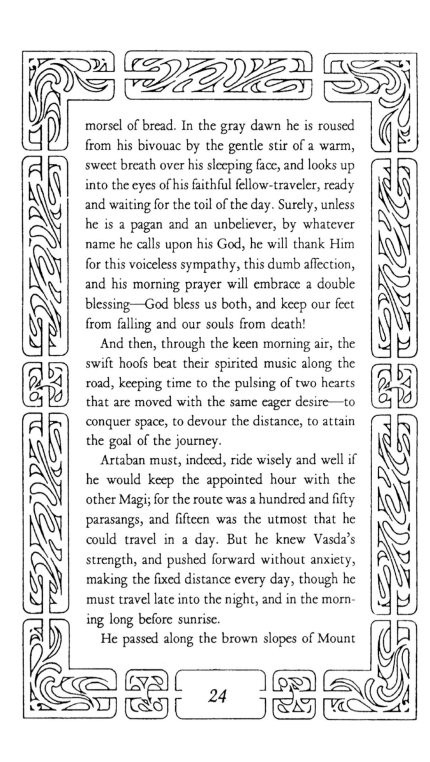

morsel of bread. In the gray dawn he is roused
from his bivouac by the gentle stir of a warm,
sweet breath over his sleeping face, and looks up
into the eyes of his faithful fellow-traveler, ready
and waiting for the toil of the day. Surely, unless
he is a pagan and an unbeliever, by whatever
name he calls upon his God, he will thank Him
for this voiceless sympathy, this dumb affection,
and his morning prayer will embrace a double
blessing—God bless us both, and keep our feet
from falling and our souls from death!

And then, through the keen morning air, the
swift hoofs beat their spirited music along the
road, keeping time to the pulsing of two hearts
that are moved with the same eager desire—to
conquer space, to devour the distance, to attain
the goal of the journey.

Artaban must, indeed, ride wisely and well if
he would keep the appointed hour with the
other Magi; for the route was a hundred and fifty
parasangs, and fifteen was the utmost that he
could travel in a day. But he knew Vasda's
strength, and pushed forward without anxiety,
making the fixed distance every day, though he
must travel late into the night, and in the morning long before sunrise.

He passed along the brown slopes of Mount

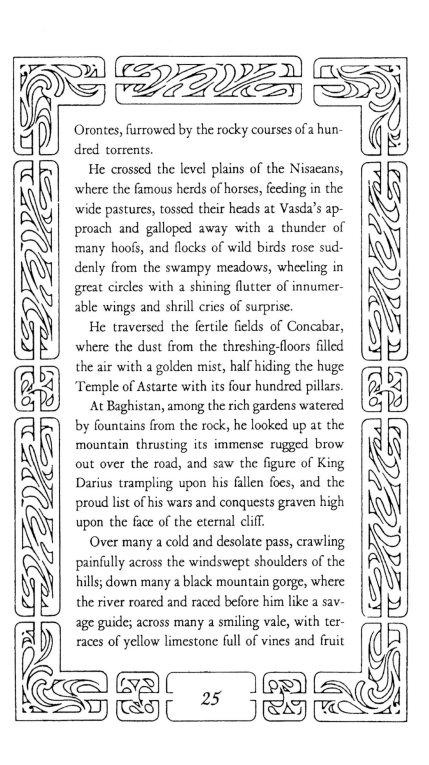

Orontes, furrowed by the rocky courses of a hundred torrents.

He crossed the level plains of the Nisaeans, where the famous herds of horses, feeding in the wide pastures, tossed their heads at Vasda's approach and galloped away with a thunder of many hoofs, and flocks of wild birds rose suddenly from the swampy meadows, wheeling in great circles with a shining flutter of innumerable wings and shrill cries of surprise.

He traversed the fertile fields of Concabar, where the dust from the threshing-floors filled the air with a golden mist, half hiding the huge Temple of Astarte with its four hundred pillars.

At Baghistan, among the rich gardens watered by fountains from the rock, he looked up at the mountain thrusting its immense rugged brow out over the road, and saw the figure of King Darius trampling upon his fallen foes, and the proud list of his wars and conquests graven high upon the face of the eternal cliff.

Over many a cold and desolate pass, crawling painfully across the windswept shoulders of the hills; down many a black mountain gorge, where the river roared and raced before him like a savage guide; across many a smiling vale, with terraces of yellow limestone full of vines and fruit trees; through the oak groves of Carine and the dark Gates of Zagros, walled in by precipices; into the ancient city of Chala, where the people of Samaria had been kept in captivity long ago; and out again by the mighty portal, riven through the encircling hills, where he saw the image of the High Priest of the Magi sculptured on the wall of rock, with hand uplifted as if to bless the centuries of pilgrims; past the entrance of the narrow defile, filled from end to end with orchards of peaches and figs, through which the river Gyndes foamed down to meet him; over the broad rice-fields, where the autumnal vapors spread their deathly mists; following along the course of the river, under tremulous shadows of poplar and tamarind, among the lower hills; and out upon the flat plain, where the road ran straight as an arrow through the stubble-fields and parched meadows; past the city of Ctesiphon, where the Parthian emperors reigned, and the vast metropolis of Seleucia which Alexander built; across the swirling floods of Tigris and the many channels of Euphrates, flowing yellow through the corn-lands—Artaban pressed onward until he arrived, at nightfall of the tenth day, beneath the shattered walls of populous Babylon.

Vasda was almost spent, and he would gladly have turned into the city to find rest and refreshment for himself and for her. But he knew that it was three hours' journey yet to the Temple of the Seven Spheres, and he must reach the place by midnight if he would find his comrades waiting. So he did not halt, but rode steadily across the stubble-fields.

A grove of date-palms made an island of glooms in the pale yellow sea. As she passed into the shadow Vasda slackened her pace, and began to pick her way more carefully.

Near the farther end of the darkness an access of caution seemed to fall upon her. She scented some danger or difficulty; it was not in her heart to fly from it—only to be prepared for it, and to meet it wisely as a good horse should do. The grove was close and silent as the tomb; not a leaf rustled, not a bird sang.

She felt her steps before her delicately, carrying her head low, and sighing now and then with apprehension. At last she gave a quick breath of anxiety and dismay, and stood stock-still, quivering in every muscle, before a dark object in the shadow of the last palm tree.

Artaban dismounted. The dim starlight revealed the form of a man lying across the road.

His humble dress and the outline of his haggard face showed that he was probably one of the poor Hebrew exiles who still dwelt in great numbers in the vicinity. His pallid skin, dry and yellow as parchment, bore the mark of the deadly fever which ravaged the marshlands in autumn. The chill of death was in his lean hand, and, as Artaban released it, the arm fell back inertly upon the motionless breast.

He turned away with a thought of pity, consigning the body to that strange burial which the Magians deemed most fitting—the funeral of the desert, from which the kites and vultures rise on dark wings, and the beasts of prey slink furtively away, leaving only a heap of white bones in the sand.

But, as he turned, a long, faint, ghostly sigh came from the man's lips. The brown, bony fingers closed convulsively on the hem of the Magian's robe and held him fast.

Artaban's heart leaped to his throat, not with fear, but with a dumb resentment at the importunity of this blind delay.

How could he stay here in the darkness to minister to a dying stranger? What claim had this unknown fragment of human life upon his compassion or his service? If he lingered but for

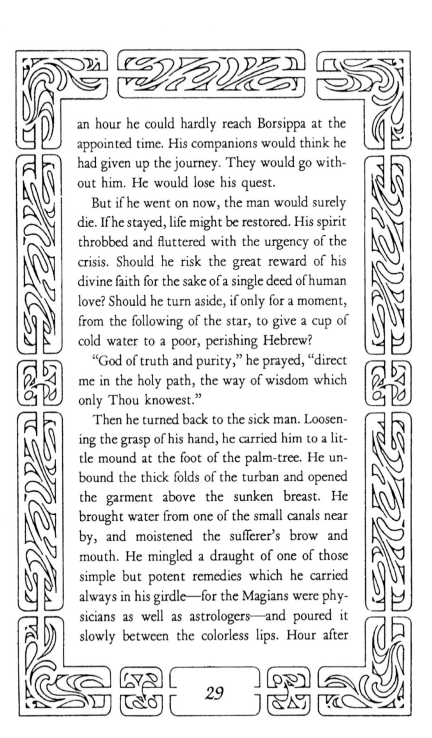

an hour he could hardly reach Borsippa at the appointed time. His companions would think he had given up the journey. They would go without him. He would lose his quest.

But if he went on now, the man would surely die. If he stayed, life might be restored. His spirit throbbed and fluttered with the urgency of the crisis. Should he risk the great reward of his divine faith for the sake of a single deed of human love? Should he turn aside, if only for a moment, from the following of the star, to give a cup of cold water to a poor, perishing Hebrew?

"God of truth and purity," he prayed, "direct me in the holy path, the way of wisdom which only Thou knowest."

Then he turned back to the sick man. Loosening the grasp of his hand, he carried him to a little mound at the foot of the palm-tree. He unbound the thick folds of the turban and opened the garment above the sunken breast. He brought water from one of the small canals near by, and moistened the sufferer's brow and mouth. He mingled a draught of one of those simple but potent remedies which he carried always in his girdle—for the Magians were physicians as well as astrologers—and poured it slowly between the colorless lips. Hour after

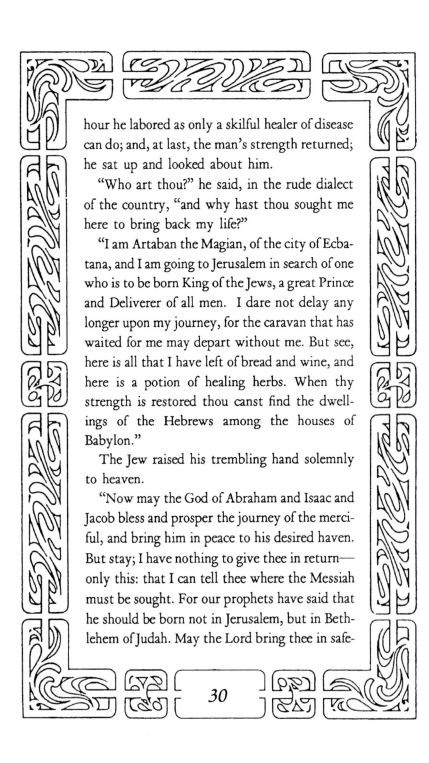

hour he labored as only a skilful healer of disease can do; and, at last, the man's strength returned; he sat up and looked about him.

"Who art thou?" he said, in the rude dialect of the country, "and why hast thou sought me here to bring back my life?"

"I am Artaban the Magian, of the city of Ecbatana, and I am going to Jerusalem in search of one who is to be born King of the Jews, a great Prince and Deliverer of all men. I dare not delay any longer upon my journey, for the caravan that has waited for me may depart without me. But see, here is all that I have left of bread and wine, and here is a potion of healing herbs. When thy strength is restored thou canst find the dwellings of the Hebrews among the houses of Babylon."

The Jew raised his trembling hand solemnly to heaven.

"Now may the God of Abraham and Isaac and Jacob bless and prosper the journey of the merciful, and bring him in peace to his desired haven. But stay; I have nothing to give thee in return—only this: that I can tell thee where the Messiah must be sought. For our prophets have said that he should be born not in Jerusalem, but in Bethlehem of Judah. May the Lord bring thee in safe-

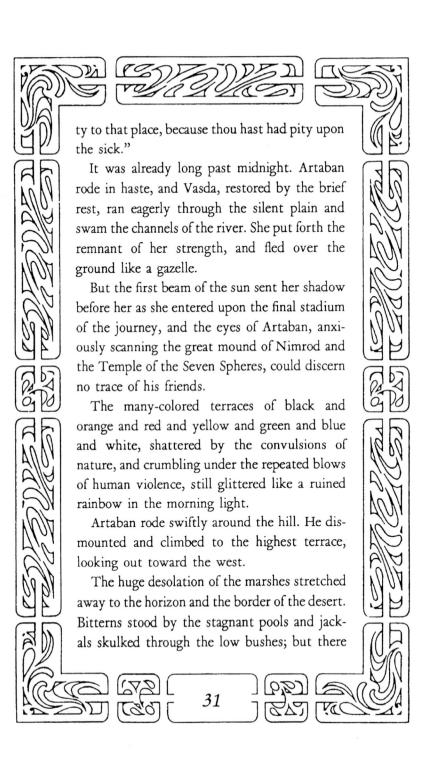

ty to that place, because thou hast had pity upon the sick."

It was already long past midnight. Artaban rode in haste, and Vasda, restored by the brief rest, ran eagerly through the silent plain and swam the channels of the river. She put forth the remnant of her strength, and fled over the ground like a gazelle.

But the first beam of the sun sent her shadow before her as she entered upon the final stadium of the journey, and the eyes of Artaban, anxiously scanning the great mound of Nimrod and the Temple of the Seven Spheres, could discern no trace of his friends.

The many-colored terraces of black and orange and red and yellow and green and blue and white, shattered by the convulsions of nature, and crumbling under the repeated blows of human violence, still glittered like a ruined rainbow in the morning light.

Artaban rode swiftly around the hill. He dismounted and climbed to the highest terrace, looking out toward the west.

The huge desolation of the marshes stretched away to the horizon and the border of the desert. Bitterns stood by the stagnant pools and jackals skulked through the low bushes; but there

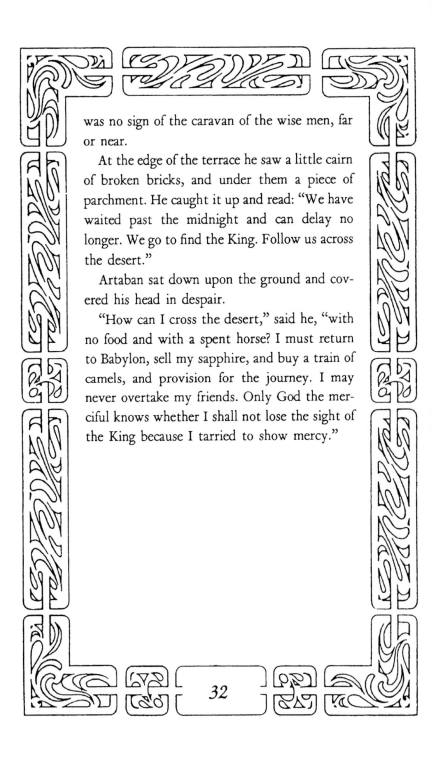

was no sign of the caravan of the wise men, far or near.

At the edge of the terrace he saw a little cairn of broken bricks, and under them a piece of parchment. He caught it up and read: "We have waited past the midnight and can delay no longer. We go to find the King. Follow us across the desert."

Artaban sat down upon the ground and covered his head in despair.

"How can I cross the desert," said he, "with no food and with a spent horse? I must return to Babylon, sell my sapphire, and buy a train of camels, and provision for the journey. I may never overtake my friends. Only God the merciful knows whether I shall not lose the sight of the King because I tarried to show mercy."

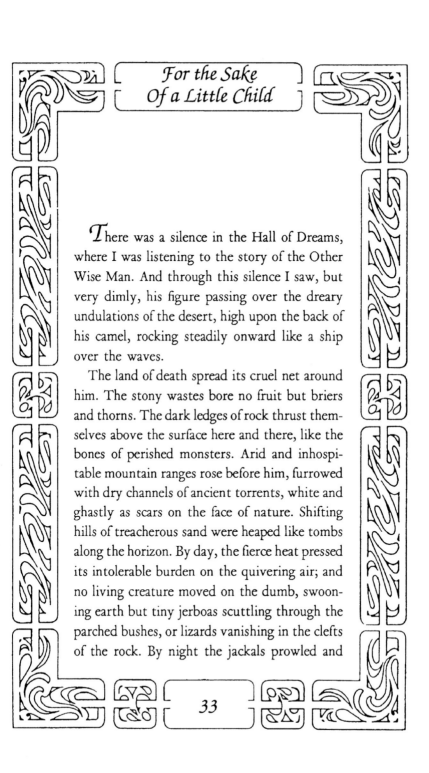

For the Sake
Of a Little Child

There was a silence in the Hall of Dreams, where I was listening to the story of the Other Wise Man. And through this silence I saw, but very dimly, his figure passing over the dreary undulations of the desert, high upon the back of his camel, rocking steadily onward like a ship over the waves.

The land of death spread its cruel net around him. The stony wastes bore no fruit but briers and thorns. The dark ledges of rock thrust themselves above the surface here and there, like the bones of perished monsters. Arid and inhospitable mountain ranges rose before him, furrowed with dry channels of ancient torrents, white and ghastly as scars on the face of nature. Shifting hills of treacherous sand were heaped like tombs along the horizon. By day, the fierce heat pressed its intolerable burden on the quivering air; and no living creature moved on the dumb, swooning earth but tiny jerboas scuttling through the parched bushes, or lizards vanishing in the clefts of the rock. By night the jackals prowled and

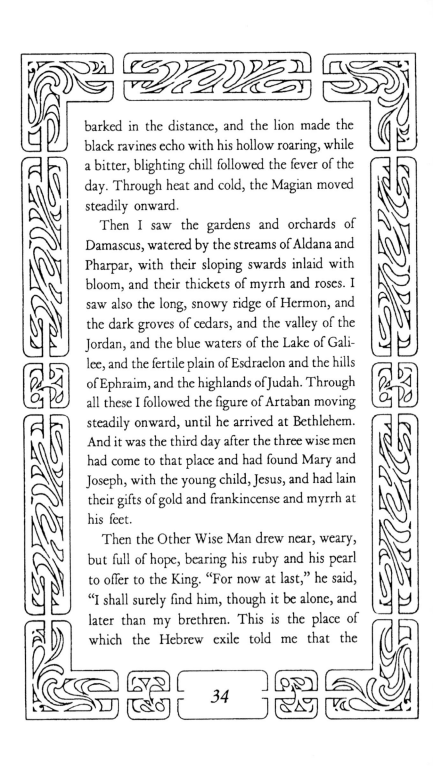

barked in the distance, and the lion made the black ravines echo with his hollow roaring, while a bitter, blighting chill followed the fever of the day. Through heat and cold, the Magian moved steadily onward.

Then I saw the gardens and orchards of Damascus, watered by the streams of Aldana and Pharpar, with their sloping swards inlaid with bloom, and their thickets of myrrh and roses. I saw also the long, snowy ridge of Hermon, and the dark groves of cedars, and the valley of the Jordan, and the blue waters of the Lake of Galilee, and the fertile plain of Esdraelon and the hills of Ephraim, and the highlands of Judah. Through all these I followed the figure of Artaban moving steadily onward, until he arrived at Bethlehem. And it was the third day after the three wise men had come to that place and had found Mary and Joseph, with the young child, Jesus, and had lain their gifts of gold and frankincense and myrrh at his feet.

Then the Other Wise Man drew near, weary, but full of hope, bearing his ruby and his pearl to offer to the King. "For now at last," he said, "I shall surely find him, though it be alone, and later than my brethren. This is the place of which the Hebrew exile told me that the

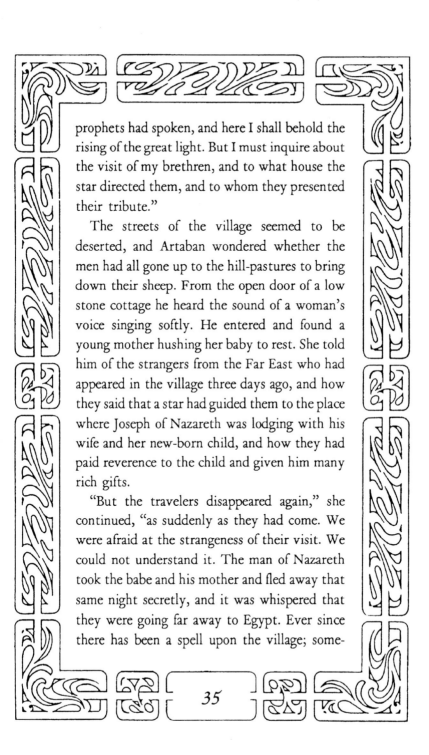

prophets had spoken, and here I shall behold the rising of the great light. But I must inquire about the visit of my brethren, and to what house the star directed them, and to whom they presented their tribute."

The streets of the village seemed to be deserted, and Artaban wondered whether the men had all gone up to the hill-pastures to bring down their sheep. From the open door of a low stone cottage he heard the sound of a woman's voice singing softly. He entered and found a young mother hushing her baby to rest. She told him of the strangers from the Far East who had appeared in the village three days ago, and how they said that a star had guided them to the place where Joseph of Nazareth was lodging with his wife and her new-born child, and how they had paid reverence to the child and given him many rich gifts.

"But the travelers disappeared again," she continued, "as suddenly as they had come. We were afraid at the strangeness of their visit. We could not understand it. The man of Nazareth took the babe and his mother and fled away that same night secretly, and it was whispered that they were going far away to Egypt. Ever since there has been a spell upon the village; something evil hangs over it. They say that the Roman soldiers are coming from Jerusalem to force a new tax from us, and the men have driven the flocks and herds far back among the hills, and hidden themselves to escape it."

Artaban listened to her gentle, timid speech and the child in her arms looked up in his face and smiled, stretching out its rosy hands to grasp at the winged circle of gold on his breast. His heart warmed to the touch. It seemed like a greeting of love and trust to one who had journeyed long in loneliness and perplexity, fighting with his own doubts and fears, and following a light that was veiled in clouds.

"Might not this child have been the promised Prince?" he asked within himself, as he touched its soft cheek. "Kings have been born ere now in lowlier houses than this, and the favorite of the stars may rise even from a cottage. But it has not seemed good to the God of wisdom to reward my search so soon and so easily. The one whom I seek has gone before me; and now I must follow the King of Egypt."

The young mother laid the babe in its cradle, and rose to minister to the wants of the strange guest that fate had brought into her house. She set food before him, the plain fare of peasants,

but willingly offered, and therefore full of refreshment for the soul as well as for the body.
Artaban accepted it gratefully; and, as he ate, the
child fell into a happy slumber, and murmured
sweetly in its dreams, and a great peace filled the
quiet room.

But suddenly there came the noise of a wild
confusion and uproar in the streets of the village,
a shrieking and wailing of women's voices, a
clangor of swords, and a desperate cry: "The
soldiers! the soldiers of Herod! They are killing
our children."

The young mother's face grew white with terror. She clasped her child to her bosom, and
crouched motionless in the darkest corner of the
room, covering him with the folds of her robe,
lest he should wake and cry.

But Artaban went quickly and stood in the
doorway of the house. His broad shoulders filled
the portal from side to side, and the peak of his
white cap all but touched the lintel.

The soldiers came hurrying down the street
with bloody hands and dripping swords. At the
sight of the stranger in his imposing dress they
hesitated with surprise. The captain of the band
approached the threshold to thrust him aside.
But Artaban did not stir. His face was as calm

as though he were watching the stars, and in his eyes there burned that steady radiance before which even the half-tamed hunting leopard shrinks and the fierce bloodhound pauses in his leap. He held the soldier silently for an instant, and then said, in a low voice:

"I am all alone in this place, and I am waiting to give this jewel to the prudent captain who will leave me in peace."

He showed the ruby, glistening in the hollow of his hand like a great drop of blood.

The captain was amazed at the splendor of the gem. The pupils of his eyes expanded with desire, and the hard lines of greed wrinkled around his lips. He stretched out his hand and took the ruby.

"March on!" he cried to his men. "There is no child here. The house is still."

The clamor and the clang of arms passed down the street as the headlong fury of the chase sweeps by the secret covert where the trembling deer is hidden. Artaban re-entered the cottage. He turned his face to the east and prayed:

"God of truth, forgive my sin! I have said the thing that is not, to save the life of a child. And two of my gifts are gone. I have spent for man that which was meant for God. Shall I ever be worthy to see the face of the King?"

But the voice of the woman, weeping for joy in the shadow behind him, said, very gently:

"Because thou hast saved the life of my little one, may the Lord bless thee and keep thee; the Lord make His face to shine upon thee and be gracious unto thee; the Lord lift up His countenance upon thee and give thee peace."

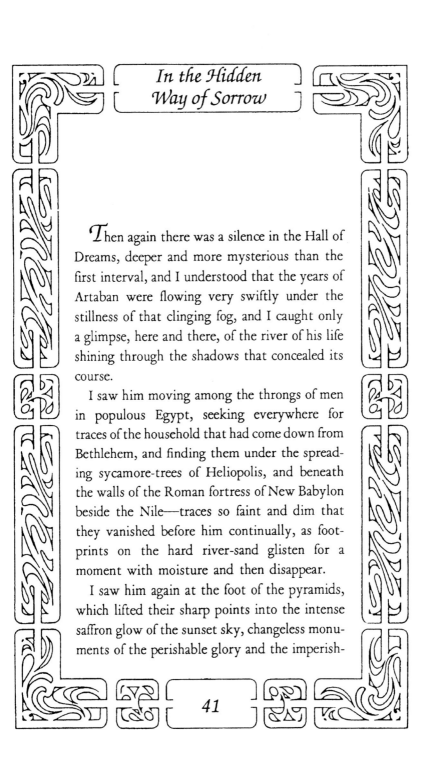

In the Hidden Way of Sorrow

*T*hen again there was a silence in the Hall of Dreams, deeper and more mysterious than the first interval, and I understood that the years of Artaban were flowing very swiftly under the stillness of that clinging fog, and I caught only a glimpse, here and there, of the river of his life shining through the shadows that concealed its course.

I saw him moving among the throngs of men in populous Egypt, seeking everywhere for traces of the household that had come down from Bethlehem, and finding them under the spreading sycamore-trees of Heliopolis, and beneath the walls of the Roman fortress of New Babylon beside the Nile—traces so faint and dim that they vanished before him continually, as footprints on the hard river-sand glisten for a moment with moisture and then disappear.

I saw him again at the foot of the pyramids, which lifted their sharp points into the intense saffron glow of the sunset sky, changeless monuments of the perishable glory and the imperishable hope of man. He looked up into the vast countenance of the crouching Sphinx and vainly tried to read the meaning of the calm eyes and smiling mouth. Was it, indeed, the mockery of all effort and all aspiration, as Tigranes had said—the cruel jest of a riddle that has no answer, a search that never can succeed? or was there a touch of pity and encouragement in that inscrutable smile—a promise that even the defeated should attain a victory, and the disappointed should discover a prize, and the ignorant should be made wise, and the blind should see, and the wandering should come into the haven at last?

I saw him again in an obscure house of Alexandria, taking counsel with a Hebrew rabbi. The venerable man, bending over the rolls of parchment on which the prophecies of Israel were written, read aloud the pathetic words which foretold the sufferings of the promised Messiah—the despised and rejected of men, the man of sorrows and the acquaintance of grief.

"And remember, my son," said he, fixing his deep-set eyes upon the face of Artaban, "the King whom you are seeking is not to be found in a palace, nor among the rich and powerful. If the light of the world and the glory of Israel had been appointed to come with the greatness of earthly splendor, it must have appeared long ago. For no son of Abraham will ever again rival the power which Joseph had in the palaces of Egypt, or the magnificence of Solomon throned between the lions in Jerusalem. But the light for which the world is waiting is a new light, the glory that shall rise out of patient and triumphant suffering. And the kingdom which is to be established forever is a new kingdom, the royalty of perfect and unconquerable love.

"I do not know how this shall come to pass, nor how the turbulent kings and peoples of earth shall be brought to acknowledge the Messiah and pay homage to him. But this I know. Those who seek Him will do well to look among the poor and the lowly, the sorrowful and the oppressed."

So I saw the Other Wise Man again and again, traveling from place to place, and searching among the people of the dispersion, with whom the little family from Bethlehem might, perhaps, have found a refuge. He passed through countries where famine lay heavy upon the land, and the poor were crying for bread. He made his dwelling in plague-stricken cities where the sick were languishing in the bitter companionship of helpless misery. He visited the oppressed and the afflicted in the gloom of subterranean prisons, and the crowded wretchedness of slave-markets, and the weary toil of galley-ships. In all this populous and intricate world of anguish, though he found none to worship, he found many to help. He fed the hungry, and clothed the naked, and healed the sick, and comforted the captive; and his years went by more swiftly than the weaver's shuttle that flashes back and forth through the loom while the web grows and the invisible pattern is completed.

It seemed almost as if he had forgotten his quest. But once I saw him for a moment as he stood alone at sunrise, waiting at the gate of a Roman prison. He had taken from a secret resting-place in his bosom the pearl, the last of his jewels. As he looked at it, a mellower luster, a soft and iridescent light, full of shifting gleams of azure and rose, trembled upon its surface. It seemed to have absorbed some reflection of the colors of the lost sapphire and ruby. So the profound, secret purpose of a noble life draws into itself the memories of past joy and past sorrow. All that has helped it, all that has hindered it, is transfused by a subtle magic into its very essence. It becomes more luminous and precious

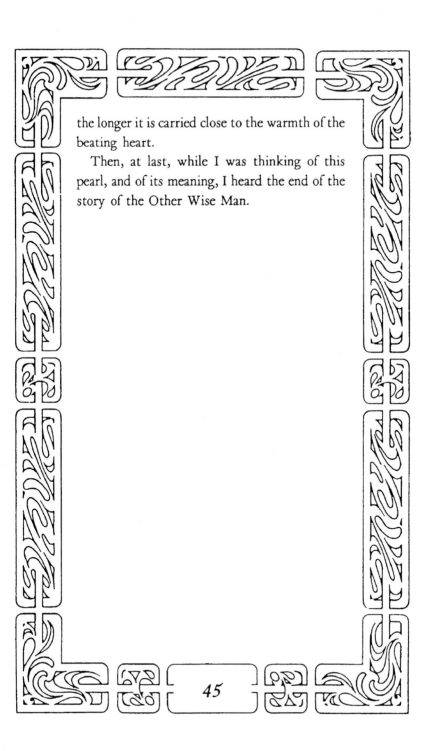

the longer it is carried close to the warmth of the beating heart.

Then, at last, while I was thinking of this pearl, and of its meaning, I heard the end of the story of the Other Wise Man.

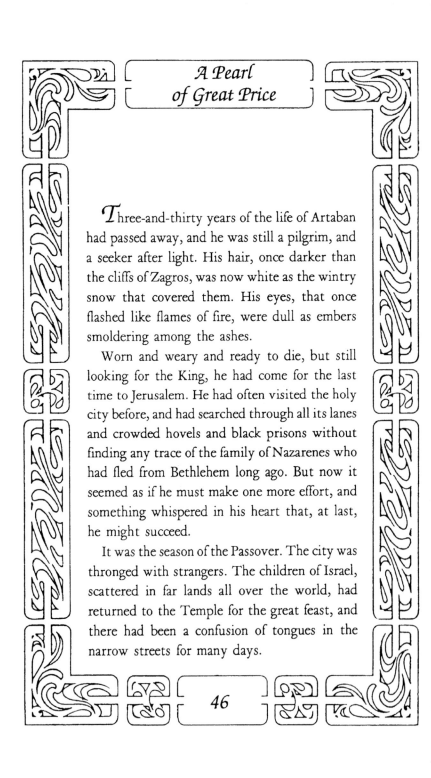

A Pearl of Great Price

*T*hree-and-thirty years of the life of Artaban had passed away, and he was still a pilgrim, and a seeker after light. His hair, once darker than the cliffs of Zagros, was now white as the wintry snow that covered them. His eyes, that once flashed like flames of fire, were dull as embers smoldering among the ashes.

Worn and weary and ready to die, but still looking for the King, he had come for the last time to Jerusalem. He had often visited the holy city before, and had searched through all its lanes and crowded hovels and black prisons without finding any trace of the family of Nazarenes who had fled from Bethlehem long ago. But now it seemed as if he must make one more effort, and something whispered in his heart that, at last, he might succeed.

It was the season of the Passover. The city was thronged with strangers. The children of Israel, scattered in far lands all over the world, had returned to the Temple for the great feast, and there had been a confusion of tongues in the narrow streets for many days.

But on this day there was a singular agitation visible in the multitude. The sky was veiled with a portentous gloom, and currents of excitement seemed to flash through the crowd like the thrill which shakes the forest on the eve of a storm. A secret tide was sweeping them all one way. The clatter of sandals, and the soft, thick sound of thousands of bare feet shuffling over the stones, flowed unceasingly along the street that leads to the Damascus gate.

Artaban joined company with a group of people from his own country, Parthian Jews who had come up to keep the Passover, and inquired of them the cause of the tumult, and where they were going.

"We are going," they answered, "to the place called Golgotha, outside the city walls, where there is to be an execution. Have you not heard what has happened? Two famous robbers are to be crucified, and with them another, called Jesus of Nazareth, a man who has done many wonderful works among the people, so that they love him greatly. But the priests and elders have said that he must die, because he gave himself out to be the Son of God. And Pilate has sent him to the cross because he said that he was the 'King of the Jews.' "

How strangely these familiar words fell upon the tired heart of Artaban! They had led him for a lifetime over land and sea. And now they came to him darkly and mysteriously like a message of despair. The King had arisen, but He had been denied and cast out. He was about to perish. Perhaps He was already dying. Could it be the same who had been born in Bethlehem thirty-three years ago, at whose birth the star had appeared in heaven, and of whose coming the prophets had spoken?

Artaban's heart beat unsteadily with that troubled, doubtful apprehension which is the excitement of old age. But he said within himself: "The ways of God are stranger than the thoughts of men, and it may be that I shall find the King, at last, in the hands of His enemies, and shall come in time to offer my pearl for His ransom before He dies."

So the old man followed the multitude with slow and painful steps toward the Damascus gate of the city. Just beyond the entrance of the guardhouse a troop of Macedonian soldiers came down the street, dragging a young girl with torn dress and disheveled hair. As the Magian paused to look at her with compassion she broke suddenly from the hands of her tormentors and threw herself at his feet, clasping him around the knees. She had seen his white cap and the winged circle on his breast.

"Have pity on me," she cried, "and save me, for the sake of the God of Purity! I also am a daughter of the true religion which is taught by the Magi. My father was a merchant of Parthia, but he is dead, and I am seized for his debts to be sold as a slave. Save me from worse than death."

Artaban trembled.

It was the old conflict in his soul, which had come to him in the palm grove of Babylon and in the cottage at Bethlehem—the conflict between the expectation of faith and the impulse of love. Twice the gift which he had consecrated to the worship of religion had been drawn from his hand to the service of humanity. This was the third trial, the ultimate probation, the final and irrevocable choice.

Was it his great opportunity, or his last temptation? He could not tell. One thing only was clear in the darkness of his mind—it was inevitable. And does not the inevitable come from God?

One thing only was sure to his divided heart—to rescue this helpless girl would be a true deed of love. And is not love the light of the soul?

He took the pearl from his bosom. Never had it seemed so luminous, so radiant, so full of tender, living luster. He laid it in the hand of the slave.

"This is thy ransom, daughter! It is the last of my treasures which I kept for the King."

While he spoke, the darkness of the sky thickened, and shuddering tremors ran through the earth, heaving convulsively like the breast of one who struggles with mighty grief.

The walls of the houses rocked to and fro. Stones were loosened and crashed into the street. Dust-clouds filled the air. The soldiers fled in terror, reeling like drunken men. But Artaban and the girl whom he had ransomed crouched helpless beneath the wall of the Praetorium.

What had he to fear? What had he to live for? He had given away the last remnant of his tribute for the King. He had parted with the last hope of finding Him. The quest was over, and it had failed. But, even in that thought, accepted and embraced, there was peace. It was not resignation. It was not submission. It was something more profound and searching. He knew that all was well, because he had done the best that he

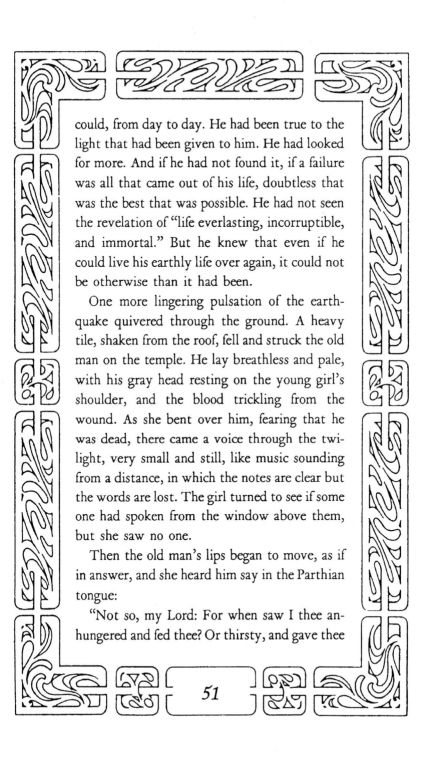

could, from day to day. He had been true to the light that had been given to him. He had looked for more. And if he had not found it, if a failure was all that came out of his life, doubtless that was the best that was possible. He had not seen the revelation of "life everlasting, incorruptible, and immortal." But he knew that even if he could live his earthly life over again, it could not be otherwise than it had been.

One more lingering pulsation of the earthquake quivered through the ground. A heavy tile, shaken from the roof, fell and struck the old man on the temple. He lay breathless and pale, with his gray head resting on the young girl's shoulder, and the blood trickling from the wound. As she bent over him, fearing that he was dead, there came a voice through the twilight, very small and still, like music sounding from a distance, in which the notes are clear but the words are lost. The girl turned to see if some one had spoken from the window above them, but she saw no one.

Then the old man's lips began to move, as if in answer, and she heard him say in the Parthian tongue:

"Not so, my Lord: For when saw I thee anhungered and fed thee? Or thirsty, and gave thee drink? When saw I thee a stranger, and took thee in? Or naked, and clothed thee? When saw I thee sick or in prison, and came unto thee? Three-and-thirty years have I looked for thee; but I have never seen thy face, nor ministered to thee, my King."

He ceased, and the sweet voice came again. And again the maid heard it, very faintly and far away. But now it seemed as though she understood the words:

"Verily I say unto thee, Inasmuch as thou hast done it unto one of the least of these my brethren, thou hast done it unto me."

A calm radiance of wonder and joy lighted the pale face of Artaban like the first ray of dawn on a snowy mountain peak. One long, last breath of relief exhaled gently from his lips.

His journey was ended. His treasures were accepted. The Other Wise Man had found the King.

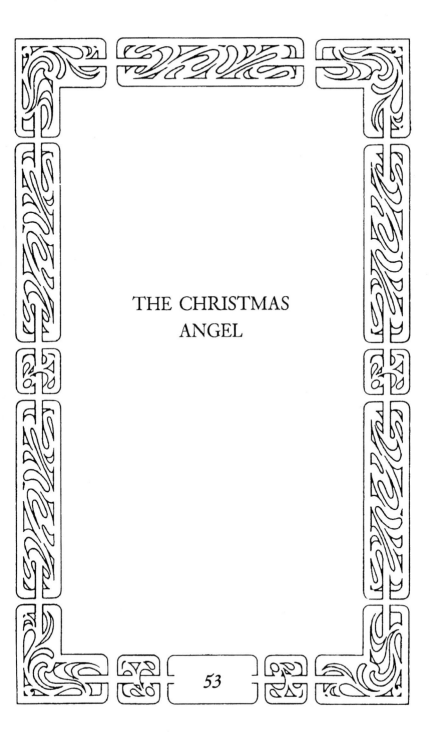

THE CHRISTMAS
ANGEL

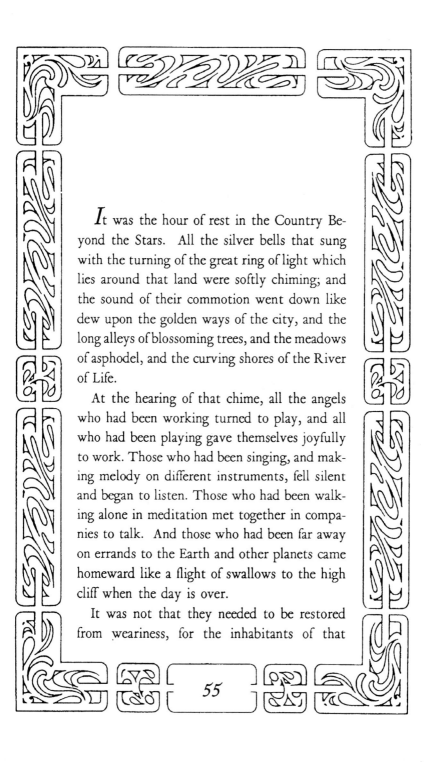

*I*t was the hour of rest in the Country Beyond the Stars. All the silver bells that sung with the turning of the great ring of light which lies around that land were softly chiming; and the sound of their commotion went down like dew upon the golden ways of the city, and the long alleys of blossoming trees, and the meadows of asphodel, and the curving shores of the River of Life.

At the hearing of that chime, all the angels who had been working turned to play, and all who had been playing gave themselves joyfully to work. Those who had been singing, and making melody on different instruments, fell silent and began to listen. Those who had been walking alone in meditation met together in companies to talk. And those who had been far away on errands to the Earth and other planets came homeward like a flight of swallows to the high cliff when the day is over.

It was not that they needed to be restored from weariness, for the inhabitants of that

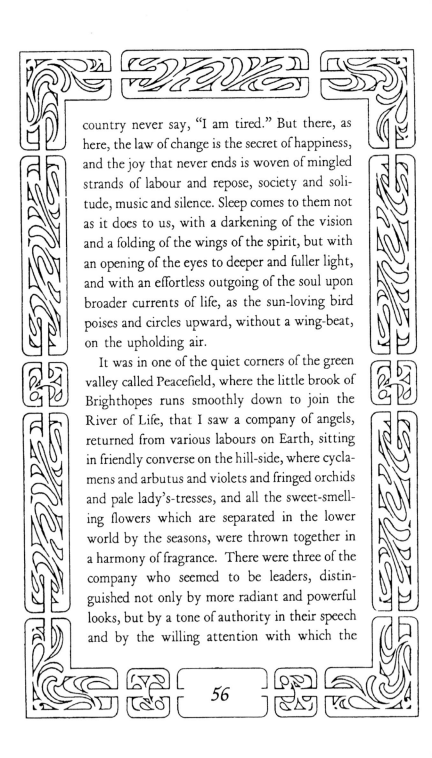

country never say, "I am tired." But there, as here, the law of change is the secret of happiness, and the joy that never ends is woven of mingled strands of labour and repose, society and solitude, music and silence. Sleep comes to them not as it does to us, with a darkening of the vision and a folding of the wings of the spirit, but with an opening of the eyes to deeper and fuller light, and with an effortless outgoing of the soul upon broader currents of life, as the sun-loving bird poises and circles upward, without a wing-beat, on the upholding air.

It was in one of the quiet corners of the green valley called Peacefield, where the little brook of Brighthopes runs smoothly down to join the River of Life, that I saw a company of angels, returned from various labours on Earth, sitting in friendly converse on the hill-side, where cyclamens and arbutus and violets and fringed orchids and pale lady's-tresses, and all the sweet-smelling flowers which are separated in the lower world by the seasons, were thrown together in a harmony of fragrance. There were three of the company who seemed to be leaders, distinguished not only by more radiant and powerful looks, but by a tone of authority in their speech and by the willing attention with which the others listened to them, as they talked of their earthly tasks, of the tangles and troubles, the wars and miseries that they had seen among men, and of the best way to get rid of them and bring sorrow to an end.

"The Earth is full of oppression and unrighteousness," said the tallest and most powerful of the angels. His voice was deep and strong, and by his shining armour and the long two-handed sword hanging over his shoulder I knew that he was the archangel Michael, the mightiest one among the warriors of the King, and the executor of the divine judgments upon the unjust. "The Earth is tormented with injustice," he cried, "and the great misery that I have seen among men is that the evil hand is often stronger than the good hand and can beat it down.

"The arm of the cruel is heavier than the arm of the kind. The unjust get the better of the just and tread on them. I have seen tyrant kings crush their helpless folk. I have seen the fields of the innocent trampled into bloody ruin by the feet of conquering armies. I have seen the wicked nation overcome the peoples that loved liberty, and take away their treasure by force of arms. I have seen poverty mocked by arrogant wealth, and purity deflowered by brute violence, and gentleness and fair-dealing bruised in the wine-press of iniquity and pride.

"There is no cure for this evil, but by the giving of greater force to the good hand. The righteous cause must be strengthened with might to resist the wicked, to defend the helpless, to punish all cruelty and unfairness, to uphold the right everywhere, and to enforce justice with unconquerable arms. Oh, that the host of Heaven might be called, arrayed, and sent to mingle in the wars of men, to make the good victorious, to destroy all evil, and to make the will of the King prevail!

"We would shake down the thrones of tyrants, and loose the bands of the oppressed. We would hold the cruel and violent with the bit of fear, and drive the greedy and fierce-minded men with the whip of terror. We would stand guard, with weapons drawn, about the innocent, the gentle, the kind, and keep the peace of God with the sword of the angels!

As he spoke, his hands were lifted to the hilt of his long blade, and he raised it above him, straight and shining, throwing sparkles of light around it, like the spray from the sharp prow of a moving ship. Bright flames of heavenly ardour leaped in the eyes of the listening angels; a martial air passed over their faces as if they longed for the call to war.

But no silver trumpet blared from the battlements of the City of God; no crimson flag was unfurled on those high secret walls; no thrilling drum-beat echoed over the smooth meadow. Only the sound of the brook of Brighthopes was heard tinkling and murmuring among the roots of the grasses and flowers; and far off a cadence of song drifted down from the inner courts of the Palace of the King.

Then another angel began to speak, and made answer to Michael. He, too, was tall and wore the look of power. But it was power of the mind rather than of the hand. His face was clear and glistening, and his eyes were lit with a steady flame which neither leaped nor fell. Of flame also were his garments, which clung about him as the fire enwraps a torch burning where there is no wind; and his great wings, spiring to a point far above his head, were like a living lamp before the altar of the Most High. By this sign I knew that it was the archangel Uriel, the spirit of the Sun, clearest in vision, deepest in wisdom of all the spirits that surround the throne.

"I hold not the same thought," said he, "as the great archangel Michael; nor, though I desire the

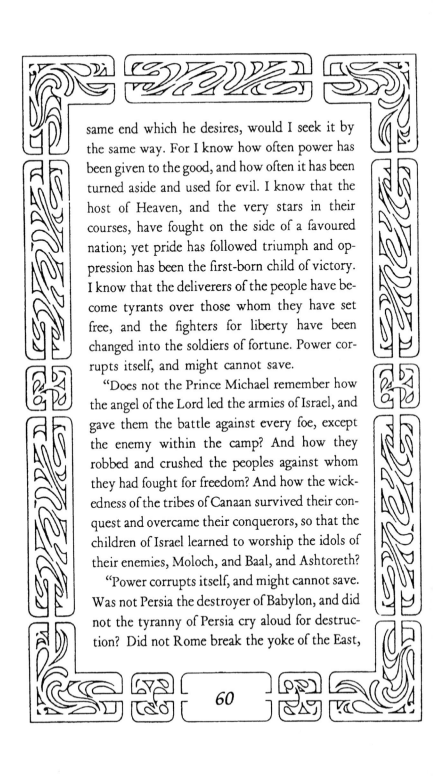

same end which he desires, would I seek it by the same way. For I know how often power has been given to the good, and how often it has been turned aside and used for evil. I know that the host of Heaven, and the very stars in their courses, have fought on the side of a favoured nation; yet pride has followed triumph and oppression has been the first-born child of victory. I know that the deliverers of the people have become tyrants over those whom they have set free, and the fighters for liberty have been changed into the soldiers of fortune. Power corrupts itself, and might cannot save.

"Does not the Prince Michael remember how the angel of the Lord led the armies of Israel, and gave them the battle against every foe, except the enemy within the camp? And how they robbed and crushed the peoples against whom they had fought for freedom? And how the wickedness of the tribes of Canaan survived their conquest and overcame their conquerors, so that the children of Israel learned to worship the idols of their enemies, Moloch, and Baal, and Ashtoreth?

"Power corrupts itself, and might cannot save. Was not Persia the destroyer of Babylon, and did not the tyranny of Persia cry aloud for destruction? Did not Rome break the yoke of the East,

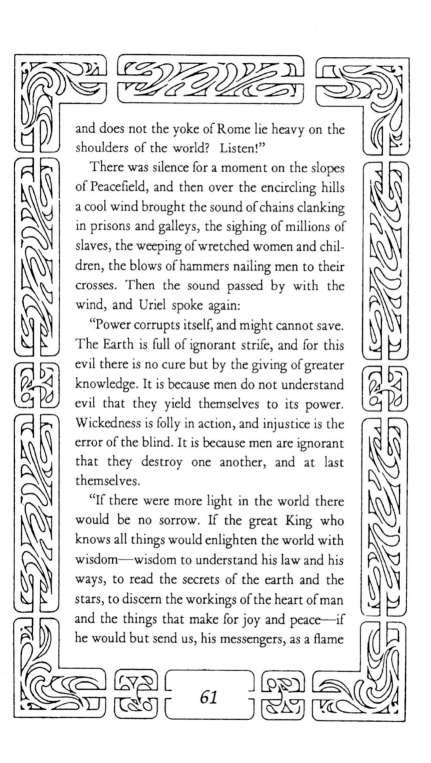

and does not the yoke of Rome lie heavy on the shoulders of the world? Listen!"

There was silence for a moment on the slopes of Peacefield, and then over the encircling hills a cool wind brought the sound of chains clanking in prisons and galleys, the sighing of millions of slaves, the weeping of wretched women and children, the blows of hammers nailing men to their crosses. Then the sound passed by with the wind, and Uriel spoke again:

"Power corrupts itself, and might cannot save. The Earth is full of ignorant strife, and for this evil there is no cure but by the giving of greater knowledge. It is because men do not understand evil that they yield themselves to its power. Wickedness is folly in action, and injustice is the error of the blind. It is because men are ignorant that they destroy one another, and at last themselves.

"If there were more light in the world there would be no sorrow. If the great King who knows all things would enlighten the world with wisdom—wisdom to understand his law and his ways, to read the secrets of the earth and the stars, to discern the workings of the heart of man and the things that make for joy and peace—if he would but send us, his messengers, as a flame

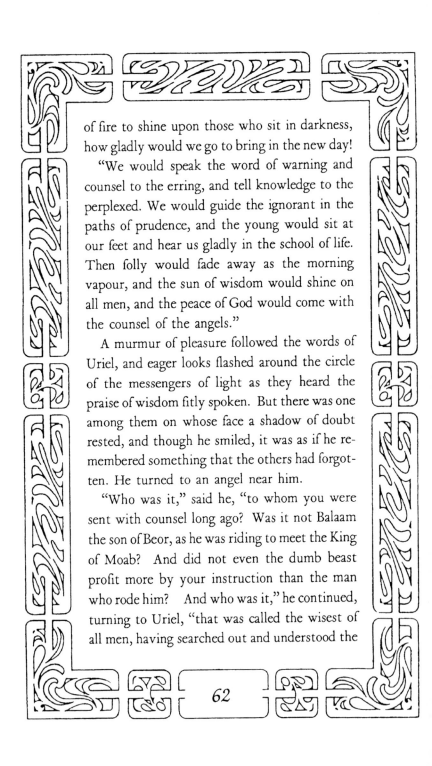

of fire to shine upon those who sit in darkness, how gladly would we go to bring in the new day!

"We would speak the word of warning and counsel to the erring, and tell knowledge to the perplexed. We would guide the ignorant in the paths of prudence, and the young would sit at our feet and hear us gladly in the school of life. Then folly would fade away as the morning vapour, and the sun of wisdom would shine on all men, and the peace of God would come with the counsel of the angels."

A murmur of pleasure followed the words of Uriel, and eager looks flashed around the circle of the messengers of light as they heard the praise of wisdom fitly spoken. But there was one among them on whose face a shadow of doubt rested, and though he smiled, it was as if he remembered something that the others had forgotten. He turned to an angel near him.

"Who was it," said he, "to whom you were sent with counsel long ago? Was it not Balaam the son of Beor, as he was riding to meet the King of Moab? And did not even the dumb beast profit more by your instruction than the man who rode him? And who was it," he continued, turning to Uriel, "that was called the wisest of all men, having searched out and understood the many inventions that are found under the sun? Was not Solomon, prince of fools and philosophers, unable by much learning to escape weariness of the flesh and despair of the spirit? Knowledge also is vanity and vexation. This I know well, because I have dwelt among men and held converse with them since the day when I was sent to instruct the first man in Eden."

Then I looked more closely at him who was speaking and recognised the beauty of the archangel Raphael, as it was pictured long ago:

"A seraph winged; six wings he wore to shade
His lineaments divine; the pair that clad
Each shoulder broad came mantling o'er his
    breast,
With regal ornament; the middle pair
Girt like a starry zone his waist, and round
Skirted his loins and thighs with downy gold
And colours dipped in Heav'n; the third his
    feet
Shadowed from either heel with feathered
    mail,
Sky-tinctured grain. Like Maia's son he stood
And shook his plumes, that Heavenly
    fragrance filled
The circuit wide."

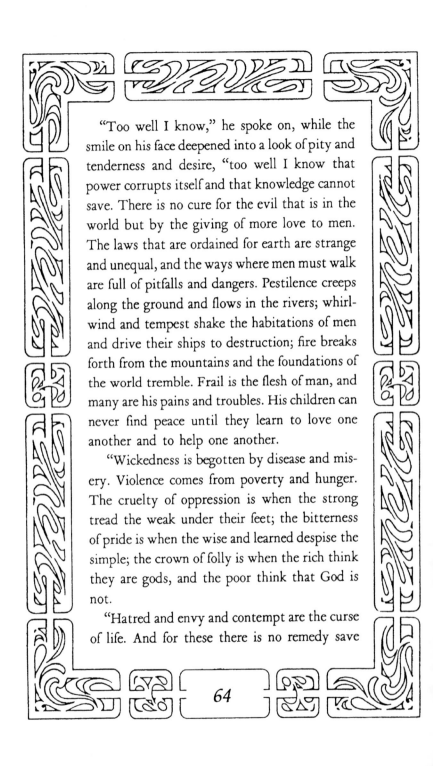

"Too well I know," he spoke on, while the smile on his face deepened into a look of pity and tenderness and desire, "too well I know that power corrupts itself and that knowledge cannot save. There is no cure for the evil that is in the world but by the giving of more love to men. The laws that are ordained for earth are strange and unequal, and the ways where men must walk are full of pitfalls and dangers. Pestilence creeps along the ground and flows in the rivers; whirlwind and tempest shake the habitations of men and drive their ships to destruction; fire breaks forth from the mountains and the foundations of the world tremble. Frail is the flesh of man, and many are his pains and troubles. His children can never find peace until they learn to love one another and to help one another.

"Wickedness is begotten by disease and misery. Violence comes from poverty and hunger. The cruelty of oppression is when the strong tread the weak under their feet; the bitterness of pride is when the wise and learned despise the simple; the crown of folly is when the rich think they are gods, and the poor think that God is not.

"Hatred and envy and contempt are the curse of life. And for these there is no remedy save

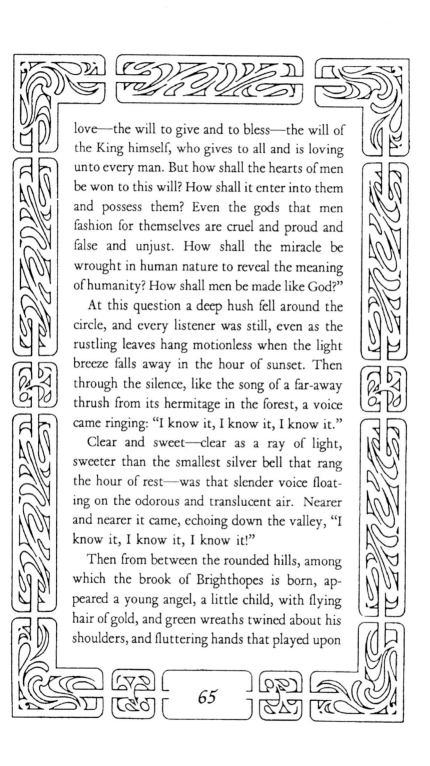

love—the will to give and to bless—the will of
the King himself, who gives to all and is loving
unto every man. But how shall the hearts of men
be won to this will? How shall it enter into them
and possess them? Even the gods that men
fashion for themselves are cruel and proud and
false and unjust. How shall the miracle be
wrought in human nature to reveal the meaning
of humanity? How shall men be made like God?"

At this question a deep hush fell around the
circle, and every listener was still, even as the
rustling leaves hang motionless when the light
breeze falls away in the hour of sunset. Then
through the silence, like the song of a far-away
thrush from its hermitage in the forest, a voice
came ringing: "I know it, I know it, I know it."

Clear and sweet—clear as a ray of light,
sweeter than the smallest silver bell that rang
the hour of rest—was that slender voice float-
ing on the odorous and translucent air. Nearer
and nearer it came, echoing down the valley, "I
know it, I know it, I know it!"

Then from between the rounded hills, among
which the brook of Brighthopes is born, appeared a young angel, a little child, with flying
hair of gold, and green wreaths twined about his
shoulders, and fluttering hands that played upon

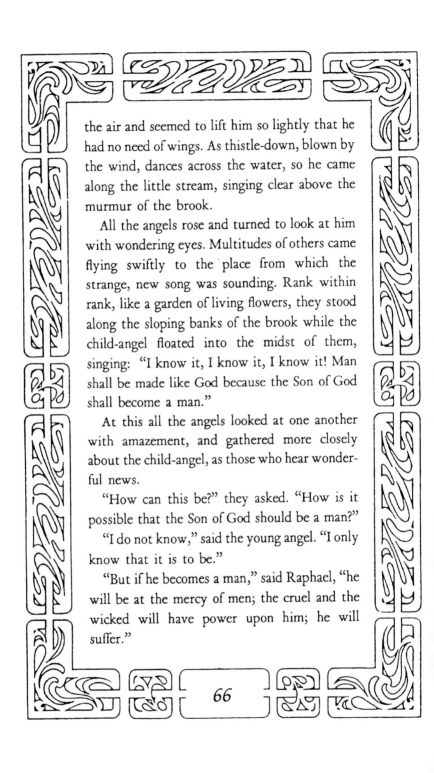

the air and seemed to lift him so lightly that he had no need of wings. As thistle-down, blown by the wind, dances across the water, so he came along the little stream, singing clear above the murmur of the brook.

All the angels rose and turned to look at him with wondering eyes. Multitudes of others came flying swiftly to the place from which the strange, new song was sounding. Rank within rank, like a garden of living flowers, they stood along the sloping banks of the brook while the child-angel floated into the midst of them, singing: "I know it, I know it, I know it! Man shall be made like God because the Son of God shall become a man."

At this all the angels looked at one another with amazement, and gathered more closely about the child-angel, as those who hear wonderful news.

"How can this be?" they asked. "How is it possible that the Son of God should be a man?"

"I do not know," said the young angel. "I only know that it is to be."

"But if he becomes a man," said Raphael, "he will be at the mercy of men; the cruel and the wicked will have power upon him; he will suffer."

"I know it," answered the young angel, "and by suffering he will understand the meaning of all sorrow and pain; and he will be able to comfort every one who cries; and his own tears will be for the healing of sad hearts; and those who are healed by him will learn for his sake to be kind to each other."

"But if the Son of God is a true man," said Uriel, "he must first be a child, simple, and lowly, and helpless. It may be that he will never gain the learning of the schools. The masters of earthly wisdom will despise him and speak scorn of him."

"I know it," said the young angel, "but in meekness will he answer them; and to those who become as little children he will give the heavenly wisdom that comes, without seeking, to the pure and gentle of heart."

"But if he becomes a man," said Michael, "evil men will hate and persecute him: they may even take his life, if they are stronger than he."

"I know it," answered the young angel, "they will nail him to a cross. But when he is lifted up, he will draw all men unto him, for he will still be the Son of God, and no heart that is open to love can help loving him, since his love for men is so great that he is willing to die for them."

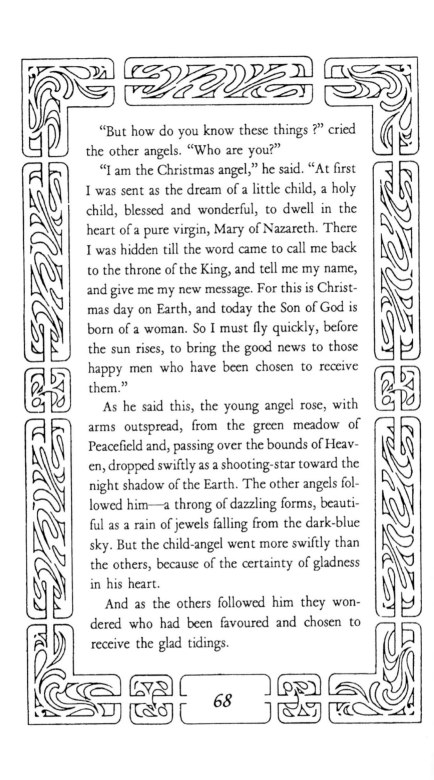

"But how do you know these things?" cried the other angels. "Who are you?"

"I am the Christmas angel," he said. "At first I was sent as the dream of a little child, a holy child, blessed and wonderful, to dwell in the heart of a pure virgin, Mary of Nazareth. There I was hidden till the word came to call me back to the throne of the King, and tell me my name, and give me my new message. For this is Christmas day on Earth, and today the Son of God is born of a woman. So I must fly quickly, before the sun rises, to bring the good news to those happy men who have been chosen to receive them."

As he said this, the young angel rose, with arms outspread, from the green meadow of Peacefield and, passing over the bounds of Heaven, dropped swiftly as a shooting-star toward the night shadow of the Earth. The other angels followed him—a throng of dazzling forms, beautiful as a rain of jewels falling from the dark-blue sky. But the child-angel went more swiftly than the others, because of the certainty of gladness in his heart.

And as the others followed him they wondered who had been favoured and chosen to receive the glad tidings.

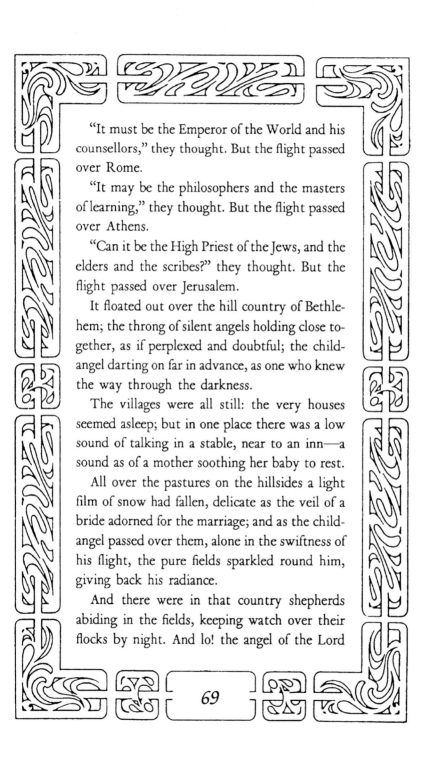

"It must be the Emperor of the World and his counsellors," they thought. But the flight passed over Rome.

"It may be the philosophers and the masters of learning," they thought. But the flight passed over Athens.

"Can it be the High Priest of the Jews, and the elders and the scribes?" they thought. But the flight passed over Jerusalem.

It floated out over the hill country of Bethlehem; the throng of silent angels holding close together, as if perplexed and doubtful; the child-angel darting on far in advance, as one who knew the way through the darkness.

The villages were all still: the very houses seemed asleep; but in one place there was a low sound of talking in a stable, near to an inn—a sound as of a mother soothing her baby to rest.

All over the pastures on the hillsides a light film of snow had fallen, delicate as the veil of a bride adorned for the marriage; and as the child-angel passed over them, alone in the swiftness of his flight, the pure fields sparkled round him, giving back his radiance.

And there were in that country shepherds abiding in the fields, keeping watch over their flocks by night. And lo! the angel of the Lord

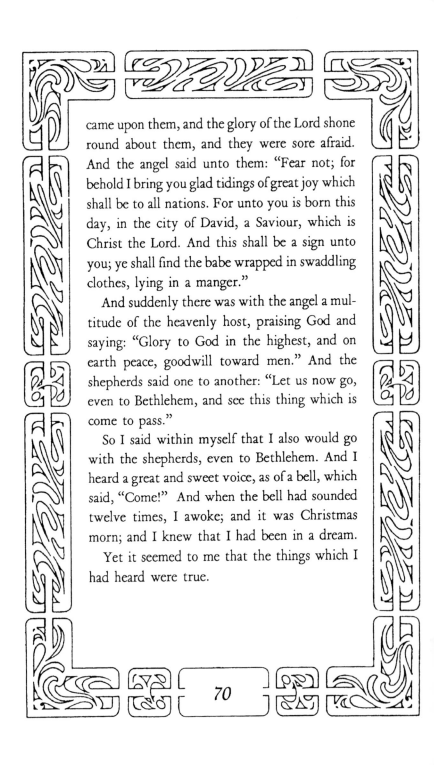

came upon them, and the glory of the Lord shone round about them, and they were sore afraid. And the angel said unto them: "Fear not; for behold I bring you glad tidings of great joy which shall be to all nations. For unto you is born this day, in the city of David, a Saviour, which is Christ the Lord. And this shall be a sign unto you; ye shall find the babe wrapped in swaddling clothes, lying in a manger."

And suddenly there was with the angel a multitude of the heavenly host, praising God and saying: "Glory to God in the highest, and on earth peace, goodwill toward men." And the shepherds said one to another: "Let us now go, even to Bethlehem, and see this thing which is come to pass."

So I said within myself that I also would go with the shepherds, even to Bethlehem. And I heard a great and sweet voice, as of a bell, which said, "Come!" And when the bell had sounded twelve times, I awoke; and it was Christmas morn; and I knew that I had been in a dream.

Yet it seemed to me that the things which I had heard were true.

THE LOST WORD

A Christmas Legend
of Long Ago

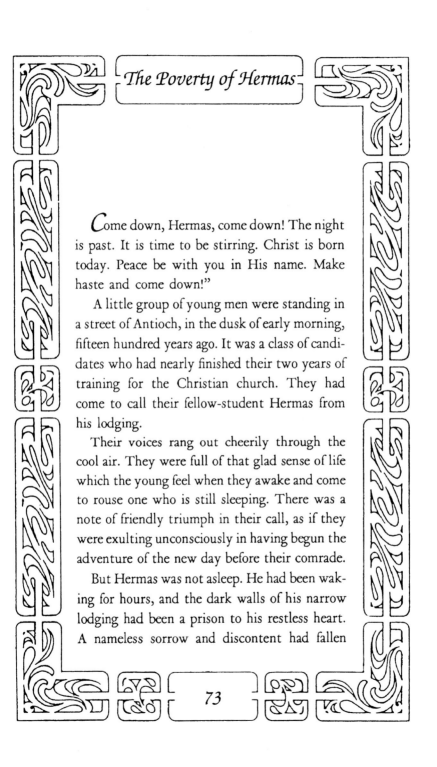

The Poverty of Hermas

Come down, Hermas, come down! The night is past. It is time to be stirring. Christ is born today. Peace be with you in His name. Make haste and come down!"

A little group of young men were standing in a street of Antioch, in the dusk of early morning, fifteen hundred years ago. It was a class of candidates who had nearly finished their two years of training for the Christian church. They had come to call their fellow-student Hermas from his lodging.

Their voices rang out cheerily through the cool air. They were full of that glad sense of life which the young feel when they awake and come to rouse one who is still sleeping. There was a note of friendly triumph in their call, as if they were exulting unconsciously in having begun the adventure of the new day before their comrade.

But Hermas was not asleep. He had been waking for hours, and the dark walls of his narrow lodging had been a prison to his restless heart. A nameless sorrow and discontent had fallen upon him, and he could find no escape from the heaviness of his own thoughts.

There is a sadness of youth into which the old cannot enter. It seems to them unreal and causeless. But it is even more bitter and burdensome than the sadness of age. There is a sting of resentment in it, a fever of angry surprise that the world should so soon be a disappointment, and life so early take on the look of a failure. It has little reason in it, perhaps, but it has all the more weariness and gloom, because the man who is oppressed by it feels dimly that it is an unnatural and an unreasonable thing, that he should be separated from the joy of his companions, and tired of living before he has fairly begun to live.

Hermas had fallen into the very depths of this strange self-pity. He was out of tune with everything around him. He had been thinking through the dead, still night, of all that he had given up when he left the house of his father, the wealthy pagan Demetrius, to join the company of the Christians. Only two years ago he had been one of the richest young men in Antioch. Now he was one of the poorest. And the worst of it was that, though he had made the choice willingly and accepted the sacrifice with a kind of enthusiasm, he was already dissatisfied with it.

The new life was no happier than the old. He was weary of vigils and fasts, weary of studies and penances, weary of prayers and sermons. He felt like a slave in a treadmill. He knew that he must go on. His honour, his conscience, his sense of duty, bound him. He could not go back to the old careless pagan life again; for something had happened within him which made a return impossible. Doubtless he had found the true religion, but he had found it only as a task and a burden; its joy and peace had slipped away from him.

He felt disillusioned and robbed. He sat beside his hard little couch, waiting without expectancy for the gray dawn of another empty day, and hardly lifting his head at the shouts of his friends.

"Come down, Hermas, you sluggard! Come down! It is Christmas morn. Awake and be glad with us!"

"I am coming," he answered listlessly; "only have patience a moment. I have been awake since midnight, and waiting for the day."

"You hear him!" said his friends one to another. "How he puts us all to shame! He is more watchful, more eager, than any of us. Our master, John the Presbyter, does well to be proud of him. He is the best man in our class. When he is baptized the church will get a strong member."

While they were talking the door opened and Hermas stepped out. He was a figure to be remarked in any company—tall, broad-shouldered, straight-hipped, with a head proudly poised on the firm column of the neck, and short brown curls clustering over the square forehead. It was the perpetual type of vigourous and intelligent young manhood, such as may be found in every century among the throngs of ordinary men, as if to show what the flower of the race should be. But the light in his dark blue eyes was clouded and uncertain; his smooth cheeks were leaner than they should have been at twenty; and there were downward lines about his mouth which spoke of desires unsatisfied and ambitions repressed. He joined his companions with brief greetings—a nod to one, a word to another—and they passed together down the steep street.

Overhead the mystery of daybreak was silently transfiguring the sky. The curtain of darkness had lifted softly upward along the edge of the horizon. The ragged crests of Mount Silpius were outlined with pale rosy light. In the central vault of heaven a few large stars twinkled drowsily. The great city, still chiefly pagan, lay more than half asleep. But multitudes of the Christians, dressed in white and carrying lighted torches in their hands, were hurrying toward the Basilica of Constantine to keep the latest holy day of the church, the new festival of the birthday of their Master.

The vast, bare building was soon crowded, and the younger converts, who were not yet permitted to stand among the baptized, found it difficult to come to their appointed place between the first two pillars of the house, just within the threshold. There was some good-humoured pressing and jostling about the door; but the candidates pushed steadily forward.

"By your leave, friends, our station is beyond you. Will you let us pass? Many thanks."

A touch here, a courteous nod there, a little patience, a little persistence, and at last they stood in their place. Hermas was taller than his companions; he could look easily over their heads and survey the white sea of people stretching away through the columns, under the shadows of the high roof, as the tide spreads on a calm day into the pillared cavern of Staffa, quiet as if the ocean hardly dared to breathe. The light of many flambeaux fell, in flickering, uncertain rays, over the assembly. At the end of the vista there was a circle of clearer, steadier radiance. Hermas could see the bishop in his great chair, surrounded by the presbyters, the lofty desks on either side for the readers of the Scripture, the communion-table and the table of offerings in the middle of the church.

The call to prayer sounded down the long aisle. Thousands of hands were joyously lifted in the air, as if the sea had blossomed into waving lilies, and the "Amen" was like the murmur of countless ripples in an echoing place.

Then the singing began, led by the choir of a hundred trained voices which the Bishop Paul had founded in Antioch. Timidly, at first, the music felt its way, as the people joined with a broken and uncertain cadence, the mingling of many little waves not yet gathered into rhythm and harmony. Soon the longer, stronger billows of song rolled in, sweeping from side to side as the men and the women answered in the clear antiphony.

Hermas had often been carried on those

"Tides of music's golden sea
Setting toward eternity."

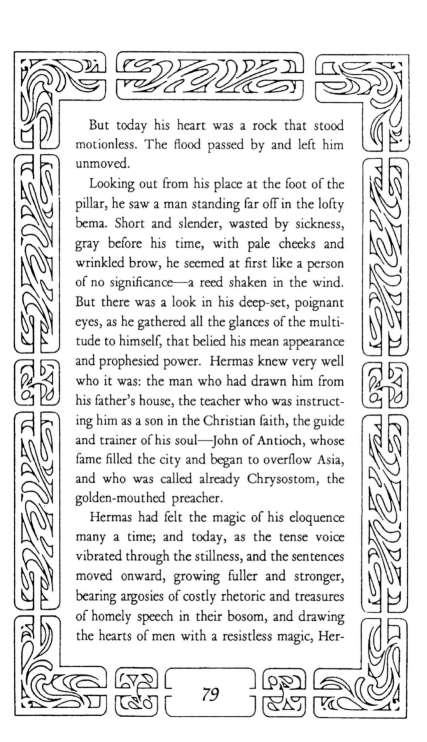

But today his heart was a rock that stood motionless. The flood passed by and left him unmoved.

Looking out from his place at the foot of the pillar, he saw a man standing far off in the lofty bema. Short and slender, wasted by sickness, gray before his time, with pale cheeks and wrinkled brow, he seemed at first like a person of no significance—a reed shaken in the wind. But there was a look in his deep-set, poignant eyes, as he gathered all the glances of the multitude to himself, that belied his mean appearance and prophesied power. Hermas knew very well who it was: the man who had drawn him from his father's house, the teacher who was instructing him as a son in the Christian faith, the guide and trainer of his soul—John of Antioch, whose fame filled the city and began to overflow Asia, and who was called already Chrysostom, the golden-mouthed preacher.

Hermas had felt the magic of his eloquence many a time; and today, as the tense voice vibrated through the stillness, and the sentences moved onward, growing fuller and stronger, bearing argosies of costly rhetoric and treasures of homely speech in their bosom, and drawing the hearts of men with a resistless magic, Her-

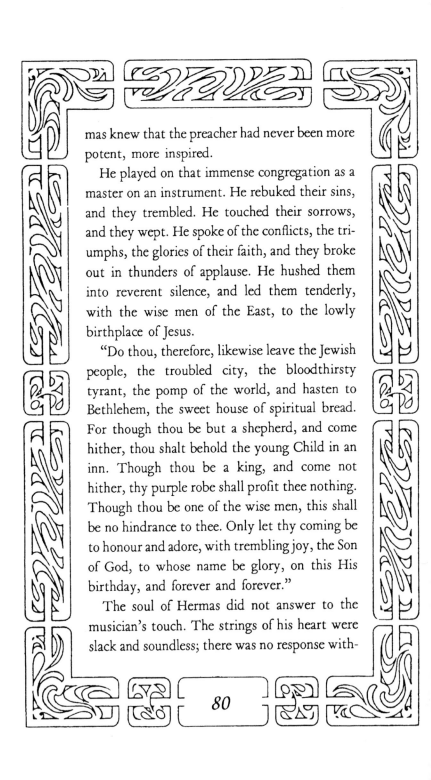

mas knew that the preacher had never been more potent, more inspired.

He played on that immense congregation as a master on an instrument. He rebuked their sins, and they trembled. He touched their sorrows, and they wept. He spoke of the conflicts, the triumphs, the glories of their faith, and they broke out in thunders of applause. He hushed them into reverent silence, and led them tenderly, with the wise men of the East, to the lowly birthplace of Jesus.

"Do thou, therefore, likewise leave the Jewish people, the troubled city, the bloodthirsty tyrant, the pomp of the world, and hasten to Bethlehem, the sweet house of spiritual bread. For though thou be but a shepherd, and come hither, thou shalt behold the young Child in an inn. Though thou be a king, and come not hither, thy purple robe shall profit thee nothing. Though thou be one of the wise men, this shall be no hindrance to thee. Only let thy coming be to honour and adore, with trembling joy, the Son of God, to whose name be glory, on this His birthday, and forever and forever."

The soul of Hermas did not answer to the musician's touch. The strings of his heart were slack and soundless; there was no response within him. He was neither shepherd, nor king, nor wise man; only an unhappy, dissatisfied, questioning youth. He was out of sympathy with the eager preacher, the joyous hearers. In their harmony he had no part. Was it for this that he had forsaken his inheritance and narrowed his life to poverty and hardship? What was it all worth?

The gracious prayers with which the young converts were blessed and dismissed before the sacrament sounded hollow in his ears. Never had he felt so utterly lonely as in that praying throng. He went out with his companions like a man departing from a banquet where all but he had been fed.

"Farewell, Hermas," they cried, as he turned from them at the door. But he did not look back, nor wave his hand. He was alone already in his heart.

When he entered the broad Avenue of the Colonnades, the sun had already topped the eastern hills, and the ruddy light was streaming through the long double row of archways and over the pavements of crimson marble. But Hermas turned his back to the morning, and walked with his shadow before him.

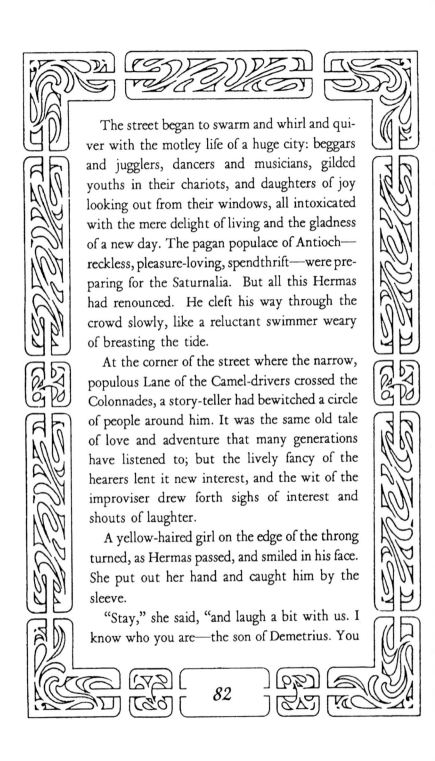

The street began to swarm and whirl and quiver with the motley life of a huge city: beggars and jugglers, dancers and musicians, gilded youths in their chariots, and daughters of joy looking out from their windows, all intoxicated with the mere delight of living and the gladness of a new day. The pagan populace of Antioch—reckless, pleasure-loving, spendthrift—were preparing for the Saturnalia. But all this Hermas had renounced. He cleft his way through the crowd slowly, like a reluctant swimmer weary of breasting the tide.

At the corner of the street where the narrow, populous Lane of the Camel-drivers crossed the Colonnades, a story-teller had bewitched a circle of people around him. It was the same old tale of love and adventure that many generations have listened to; but the lively fancy of the hearers lent it new interest, and the wit of the improviser drew forth sighs of interest and shouts of laughter.

A yellow-haired girl on the edge of the throng turned, as Hermas passed, and smiled in his face. She put out her hand and caught him by the sleeve.

"Stay," she said, "and laugh a bit with us. I know who you are—the son of Demetrius. You must have bags of gold. Why do you look so black? Love is alive yet."

Hermas shook off her hand, but not ungently.

"I don't know what you mean," he said. "You are mistaken in me. I am poorer than you are."

But as he passed on, he felt the warm touch of her fingers through the cloth on his arm. It seemed as if she had plucked him by the heart.

He went out by the Western Gate, under the golden cherubim that the Emperor Titus had stolen from the ruined Temple of Jerusalem and fixed upon the arch of triumph. He turned to the left, and climbed the hill to the road that led to the Grove of Daphne.

In all the world there was no other highway as beautiful. It wound for five miles along the foot of the mountains, among gardens and villas, plantations of myrtles and mulberries, with wide outlooks over the valley of Orontes and the distant, shimmering sea.

The richest of all the dwellings was the House of the Golden Pillars, the mansion of Demetrius. He had won the favor of the apostate Emperor Julian, whose vain efforts to restore the worship of the heathen gods, some twenty years ago, had opened an easy way to wealth and power for all who would mock and oppose Christianity.

Demetrius was not a sincere fanatic like his royal master; but he was bitter enough in his professed scorn of the new religion, to make him a favourite at the court where the old religion was in fashion. He had reaped a rich reward of his policy, and a strange sense of consistency made him more fiercely loyal to it than if it had been a real faith. He was proud of being called "the friend of Julian"; and when his son joined himself to the Christians, and acknowledged the unseen God, it seemed like an insult to his father's success. He drove the boy from his door and disinherited him.

The glittering portico of the serene, haughty house, the repose of the well-ordered garden, still blooming with belated flowers, seemed at once to deride and to invite the young outcast plodding along the dusty road. "This is your birthright," whispered the clambering rose-trees by the gate; and the closed portals of carven bronze said: "You have sold it for a thought—a dream."

A Christmas Loss

*H*ermas found the Grove of Daphne quite deserted. There was no sound in the enchanted vale but the rustling of the light winds chasing each other through the laurel thickets, and the babble of innumerable streams. Memories of the days and nights of delicate pleasure that the grove had often seen still haunted the bewildered paths and broken fountains. At the foot of a rocky eminence, crowned with the ruins of Apollo's temple, which had been mysteriously destroyed by fire just after Julian had restored and reconsecrated it, Hermas sat down beside a gushing spring, and gave himself up to sadness.

"How beautiful the world would be, how joyful, how easy to live in, without religion! These questions about unseen things, perhaps about unreal things, these restraints and duties and sacrifices—if I were only free from them all, and could only forget them all, then I could live my life as I pleased, and be happy."

"Why not?" said a quiet voice at his back. He turned, and saw an old man with a long beard and a threadbare cloak (the garb affected by the

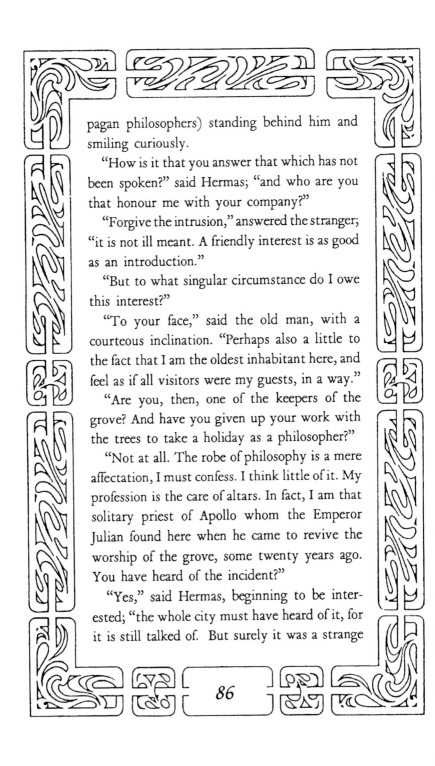

pagan philosophers) standing behind him and smiling curiously.

"How is it that you answer that which has not been spoken?" said Hermas; "and who are you that honour me with your company?"

"Forgive the intrusion," answered the stranger; "it is not ill meant. A friendly interest is as good as an introduction."

"But to what singular circumstance do I owe this interest?"

"To your face," said the old man, with a courteous inclination. "Perhaps also a little to the fact that I am the oldest inhabitant here, and feel as if all visitors were my guests, in a way."

"Are you, then, one of the keepers of the grove? And have you given up your work with the trees to take a holiday as a philosopher?"

"Not at all. The robe of philosophy is a mere affectation, I must confess. I think little of it. My profession is the care of altars. In fact, I am that solitary priest of Apollo whom the Emperor Julian found here when he came to revive the worship of the grove, some twenty years ago. You have heard of the incident?"

"Yes," said Hermas, beginning to be interested; "the whole city must have heard of it, for it is still talked of. But surely it was a strange sacrifice that you brought to celebrate the restoration of Apollo's temple?"

"You mean the goose? Well, perhaps it was not precisely what the emperor expected. But it was all that I had, and it seemed to me not inappropriate. You will agree to that if you are a Christian, as I guess from your dress."

"You speak lightly for a priest of Apollo."

"Oh, as for that, I am no bigot. The priesthood is a professional matter, and the name of Apollo is as good as any other. How many altars do you think there have been in this grove?"

"I do not know."

"Just four-and-twenty, including that of the martyr Babylas, whose ruined chapel you see just beyond us. I have had something to do with most of them in my time. They are transitory. They give employment to care-takers for a while. But the thing that lasts, and the thing that interests me, is the human life that plays around them. The game has been going on for centuries. It still disports itself very pleasantly on summer evenings through these shady walks. Believe me, for I know. Daphne and Apollo were shadows. But the flying maidens and the pursuing lovers, the music and the dances, these are the realities. Life is the game, and the world keeps it up merrily. But you? You are of a sad countenance for one so young and so fair. Are you a loser in the game?"

The words and tone of the speaker fitted Hermas' mood as a key fits the lock. He opened his heart to the old man, and told him the story of his life: his luxurious boyhood in his father's house; the irresistible spell which compelled him to forsake it when he heard John's preaching of the new religion; his lonely year with the anchorites among the mountains; the strict discipline in his teacher's house at Antioch; his weariness of duty, his distaste for poverty, his discontent with worship.

"And today," said he, "I have been thinking that I am a fool. My life is swept as bare as a hermit's cell. There is nothing in it but a dream, a thought of God, which does not satisfy me."

The singular smile deepened on his companion's face. "You are ready, then," he suggested, "to renounce your new religion and go back to that of your father?"

"No; I renounce nothing, I accept nothing. I do not wish to think about it. I only wish to live."

"A very reasonable wish, and I think you are about to see its accomplishment. Indeed, I may

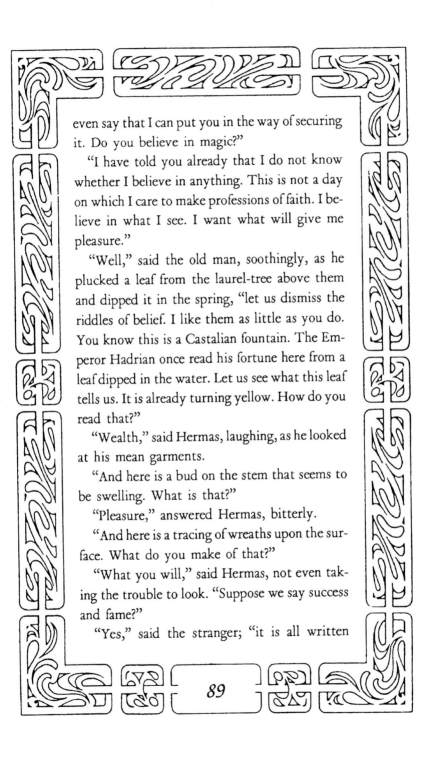

even say that I can put you in the way of securing it. Do you believe in magic?"

"I have told you already that I do not know whether I believe in anything. This is not a day on which I care to make professions of faith. I believe in what I see. I want what will give me pleasure."

"Well," said the old man, soothingly, as he plucked a leaf from the laurel-tree above them and dipped it in the spring, "let us dismiss the riddles of belief. I like them as little as you do. You know this is a Castalian fountain. The Emperor Hadrian once read his fortune here from a leaf dipped in the water. Let us see what this leaf tells us. It is already turning yellow. How do you read that?"

"Wealth," said Hermas, laughing, as he looked at his mean garments.

"And here is a bud on the stem that seems to be swelling. What is that?"

"Pleasure," answered Hermas, bitterly.

"And here is a tracing of wreaths upon the surface. What do you make of that?"

"What you will," said Hermas, not even taking the trouble to look. "Suppose we say success and fame?"

"Yes," said the stranger; "it is all written

here. I promise that you shall enjoy it all. But you do not need to believe in my promise. I am not in the habit of requiring faith of those whom I would serve. No such hard conditions for me! There is only one thing that I ask. This is the season that you Christians call the Christmas, and you have taken up the pagan custom of exchanging gifts. Well, if I give to you, you must give to me. It is a small thing, and really the thing you can best afford to part with: a single word—the name of Him you profess to worship. Let me take that word and all that belongs to it entirely out of your life, so that you shall never need to hear it or speak it again. You will be richer without it. I promise you everything, and this is all I ask in return. Do you consent?"

"Yes, I consent," said Hermas, mocking. "If you can take your price, a word, you can keep your promise, a dream."

The stranger laid the long, cool, wet leaf softly across the young man's eyes. An icicle of pain darted through them; every nerve in his body was drawn together there in a knot of agony.

Then all the tangle of pain seemed to be lifted out of him. A cool languor of delight flowed back through every vein, and he sank into a profound sleep.

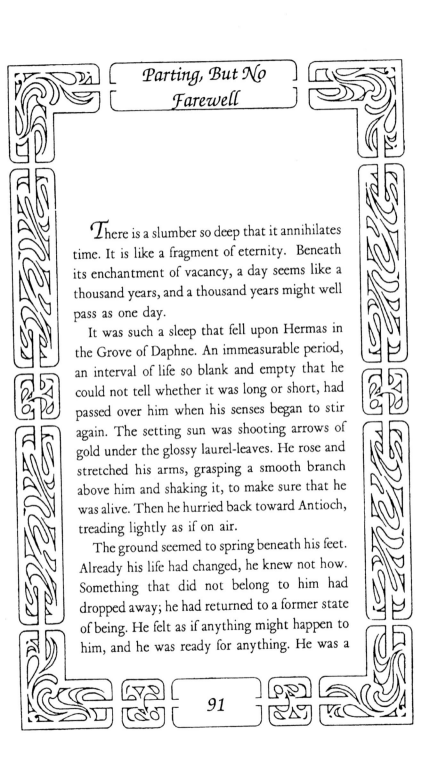

There is a slumber so deep that it annihilates time. It is like a fragment of eternity. Beneath its enchantment of vacancy, a day seems like a thousand years, and a thousand years might well pass as one day.

It was such a sleep that fell upon Hermas in the Grove of Daphne. An immeasurable period, an interval of life so blank and empty that he could not tell whether it was long or short, had passed over him when his senses began to stir again. The setting sun was shooting arrows of gold under the glossy laurel-leaves. He rose and stretched his arms, grasping a smooth branch above him and shaking it, to make sure that he was alive. Then he hurried back toward Antioch, treading lightly as if on air.

The ground seemed to spring beneath his feet. Already his life had changed, he knew not how. Something that did not belong to him had dropped away; he had returned to a former state of being. He felt as if anything might happen to him, and he was ready for anything. He was a new man, yet curiously familiar to himself—as if he had done with playing a tiresome part and returned to his natural state. He was buoyant and free, without a care, a doubt, a fear.

As he drew near to his father's house he saw a confusion of servants in the porch, and the old steward ran down to meet him at the gate.

"Lord, we have been seeking you everywhere. The master is at the point of death, and has sent for you. Since the sixth hour he calls your name continually. Come to him quickly, lord, for I fear the time is short."

Hermas entered the house at once; nothing could amaze him today. His father lay on an ivory couch in the inmost chamber, with shrunken face and restless eyes, his lean fingers picking incessantly at the silken coverlet.

"My son!" he murmured; "Hermas, my son! It is good that you have come back to me. I have missed you. I was wrong to send you away. You shall never leave me again. You are my son, my heir. I have changed everything. Hermas, my son, come nearer—close beside me. Take my hand, my son!"

The young man obeyed, and, kneeling by the couch, gathered his father's cold, twitching fingers in his firm, warm grasp. "Hermas, life is

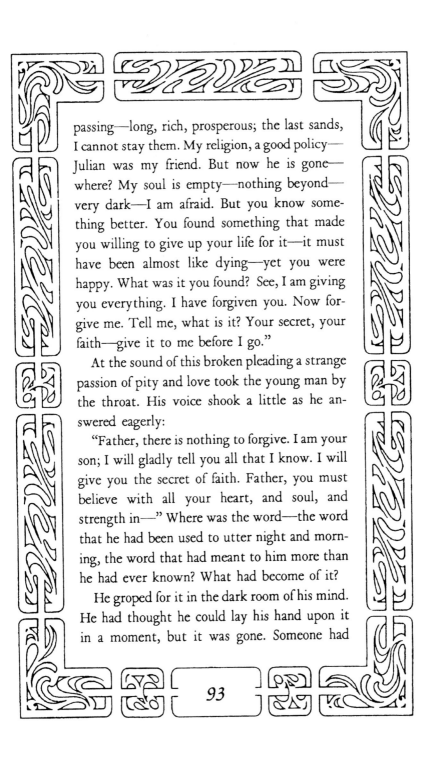

passing—long, rich, prosperous; the last sands, I cannot stay them. My religion, a good policy—Julian was my friend. But now he is gone—where? My soul is empty—nothing beyond—very dark—I am afraid. But you know something better. You found something that made you willing to give up your life for it—it must have been almost like dying—yet you were happy. What was it you found? See, I am giving you everything. I have forgiven you. Now forgive me. Tell me, what is it? Your secret, your faith—give it to me before I go."

At the sound of this broken pleading a strange passion of pity and love took the young man by the throat. His voice shook a little as he answered eagerly:

"Father, there is nothing to forgive. I am your son; I will gladly tell you all that I know. I will give you the secret of faith. Father, you must believe with all your heart, and soul, and strength in—" Where was the word—the word that he had been used to utter night and morning, the word that had meant to him more than he had ever known? What had become of it?

He groped for it in the dark room of his mind. He had thought he could lay his hand upon it in a moment, but it was gone. Someone had taken it away. Everything else was most clear to him: the terror of death; the lonely soul appealing from his father's eyes; the instant need of comfort and help. But at the one point where he looked for help he could find nothing; only an empty space. The word of hope had vanished. He felt for it blindly and in desperate haste.

"Father, wait! I have forgotten something— it has slipped away from me. I shall find it in a moment. There is hope—I will tell you presently—oh, wait!"

The bony hand gripped his like a vice; the glazed eyes opened wider. "Tell me," whispered the old man; "tell me quickly, for I must go."

The voice sank into a dull rattle. The fingers closed once more, and relaxed. The light behind the eyes went out.

Hermas, the master of the House of the Golden Pillars, was keeping watch by the dead.

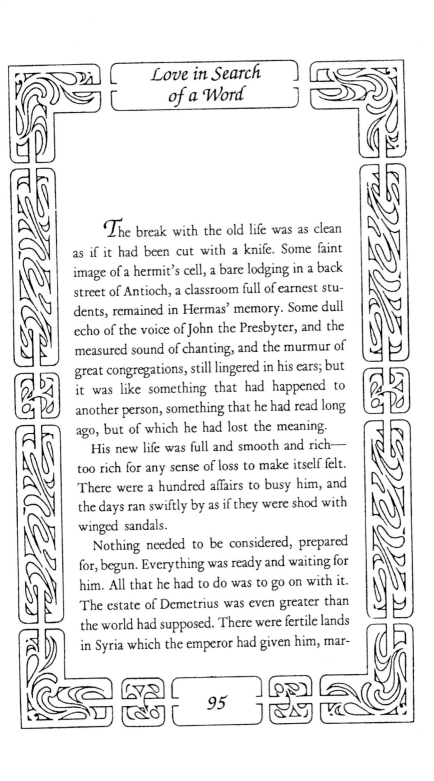

Love in Search of a Word

*T*he break with the old life was as clean as if it had been cut with a knife. Some faint image of a hermit's cell, a bare lodging in a back street of Antioch, a classroom full of earnest students, remained in Hermas' memory. Some dull echo of the voice of John the Presbyter, and the measured sound of chanting, and the murmur of great congregations, still lingered in his ears; but it was like something that had happened to another person, something that he had read long ago, but of which he had lost the meaning.

His new life was full and smooth and rich— too rich for any sense of loss to make itself felt. There were a hundred affairs to busy him, and the days ran swiftly by as if they were shod with winged sandals.

Nothing needed to be considered, prepared for, begun. Everything was ready and waiting for him. All that he had to do was to go on with it. The estate of Demetrius was even greater than the world had supposed. There were fertile lands in Syria which the emperor had given him, mar-

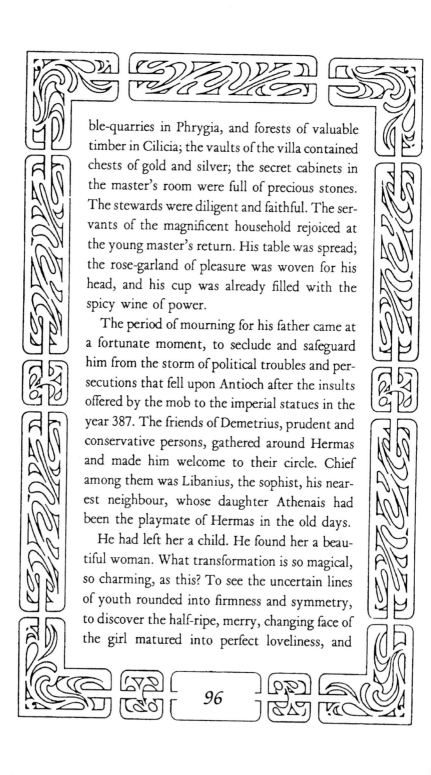

ble-quarries in Phrygia, and forests of valuable timber in Cilicia; the vaults of the villa contained chests of gold and silver; the secret cabinets in the master's room were full of precious stones. The stewards were diligent and faithful. The servants of the magnificent household rejoiced at the young master's return. His table was spread; the rose-garland of pleasure was woven for his head, and his cup was already filled with the spicy wine of power.

The period of mourning for his father came at a fortunate moment, to seclude and safeguard him from the storm of political troubles and persecutions that fell upon Antioch after the insults offered by the mob to the imperial statues in the year 387. The friends of Demetrius, prudent and conservative persons, gathered around Hermas and made him welcome to their circle. Chief among them was Libanius, the sophist, his nearest neighbour, whose daughter Athenais had been the playmate of Hermas in the old days.

He had left her a child. He found her a beautiful woman. What transformation is so magical, so charming, as this? To see the uncertain lines of youth rounded into firmness and symmetry, to discover the half-ripe, merry, changing face of the girl matured into perfect loveliness, and

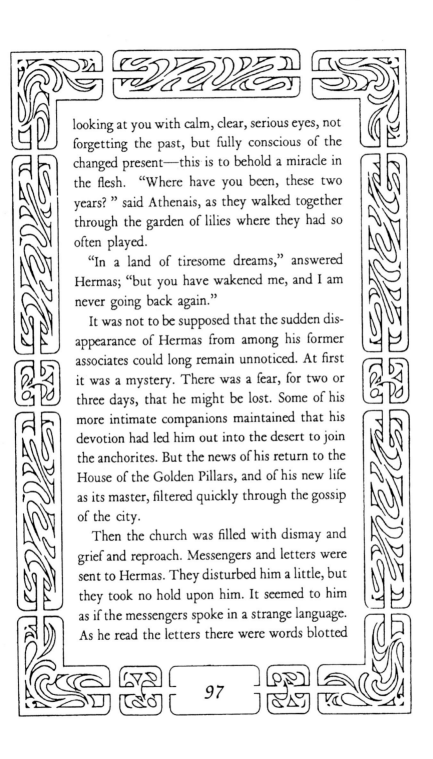

looking at you with calm, clear, serious eyes, not forgetting the past, but fully conscious of the changed present—this is to behold a miracle in the flesh. "Where have you been, these two years? " said Athenais, as they walked together through the garden of lilies where they had so often played.

"In a land of tiresome dreams," answered Hermas; "but you have wakened me, and I am never going back again."

It was not to be supposed that the sudden disappearance of Hermas from among his former associates could long remain unnoticed. At first it was a mystery. There was a fear, for two or three days, that he might be lost. Some of his more intimate companions maintained that his devotion had led him out into the desert to join the anchorites. But the news of his return to the House of the Golden Pillars, and of his new life as its master, filtered quickly through the gossip of the city.

Then the church was filled with dismay and grief and reproach. Messengers and letters were sent to Hermas. They disturbed him a little, but they took no hold upon him. It seemed to him as if the messengers spoke in a strange language. As he read the letters there were words blotted out of the writing which made the full sense unintelligible.

His old companions came to reprove him for leaving them, to warn him of the peril of apostasy, to entreat him to return. It all sounded vague and futile. They spoke as if he had betrayed or offended some one; but when they came to name the object of his fear—the one whom he had displeased, and to whom he should return—he heard nothing; there was a blur of silence in their speech. The clock pointed to the hour, but the bell did not strike. At last Hermas refused to see them any more.

One day John the Presbyter stood in the atrium. Hermas was entertaining Libanius and Athenais in the banquet-hall. When the visit of the Presbyter was announced, the young master loosed a collar of gold and jewels from his neck, and gave it to his scribe.

"Take this to John of Antioch, and tell him it is a gift from his former pupil—as a token of remembrance, or to spend for the poor of the city. I will always send him what he wants, but it is idle for us to talk together anymore. I do not understand what he says. I have not gone to the temple, nor offered sacrifice, nor denied his teaching. I have simply forgotten. I do not think

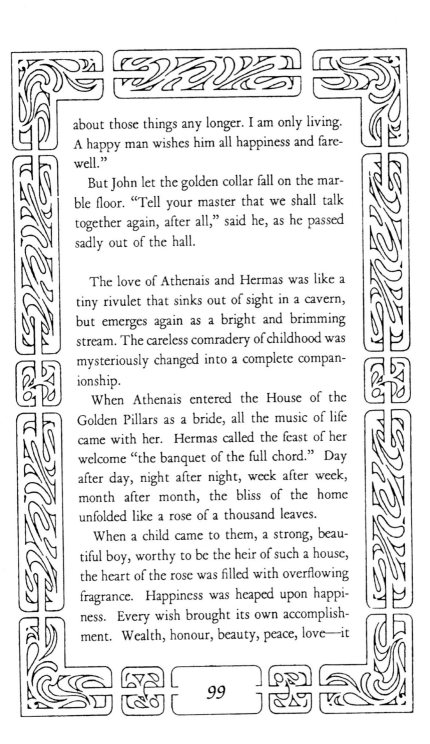

about those things any longer. I am only living. A happy man wishes him all happiness and farewell."

But John let the golden collar fall on the marble floor. "Tell your master that we shall talk together again, after all," said he, as he passed sadly out of the hall.

The love of Athenais and Hermas was like a tiny rivulet that sinks out of sight in a cavern, but emerges again as a bright and brimming stream. The careless comradery of childhood was mysteriously changed into a complete companionship.

When Athenais entered the House of the Golden Pillars as a bride, all the music of life came with her. Hermas called the feast of her welcome "the banquet of the full chord." Day after day, night after night, week after week, month after month, the bliss of the home unfolded like a rose of a thousand leaves.

When a child came to them, a strong, beautiful boy, worthy to be the heir of such a house, the heart of the rose was filled with overflowing fragrance. Happiness was heaped upon happiness. Every wish brought its own accomplishment. Wealth, honour, beauty, peace, love—it was an abundance of felicity so great that the soul of Hermas could hardly contain it.

Strangely enough, it began to press upon him, to trouble him with the very excess of joy. He felt as if there were something yet needed to complete and secure it all. There was an urgency within him, a longing to find some outlet for his feelings, he knew not how—some expression and culmination of his happiness, he knew not what.

Under his joyous demeanour a secret fire of restlessness began to burn—an expectancy of something yet to come which should put the touch of perfection on his life. He spoke of it to Athenais, as they sat together, one summer evening, in a bower of jasmine, with their boy playing at their feet. There had been music in the garden; but now the singers and lute-players had withdrawn, leaving the master and mistress alone in the lingering twilight, tremulous with inarticulate melody of unseen birds. There was a secret voice in the hour seeking vainly for utterance—a word waiting to be spoken at the centre of the charm.

"How deep is our happiness, my beloved!" said Hermas; "deeper than the sea that slumbers yonder, below the city. And yet I feel it is not quite full and perfect. There is a depth of joy that we have not yet known—a repose of happiness that is still beyond us. What is it? I have no superstitious fears, like the king who cast his signet ring into the sea because he dreaded that some secret vengeance would fall on his unbroken good fortune. That was an idle terror. But there is something that oppresses me like an invisible burden. There is something still undone, unspoken, unfelt—something that we need to complete everything. Have you not felt it, too? Can you not lead me to it?"

"Yes," she answered, lifting her eyes to his face; "I, too, have felt it, Hermas, this burden, this need, this unsatisfied longing. I think I know what it means. It is gratitude—the language of the heart, the music of happiness. There is no perfect joy without gratitude. But we have never learned it, and the want of it troubles us. It is like being dumb with a heart full of love. We must find the word for it, and say it together. Then we shall be perfectly joined in perfect joy. Come, my dear lord, let us take the boy with us, and give thanks."

Hermas lifted the child in his arms, and turned with Athenais into the depth of the garden. There was a dismantled shrine of some for-

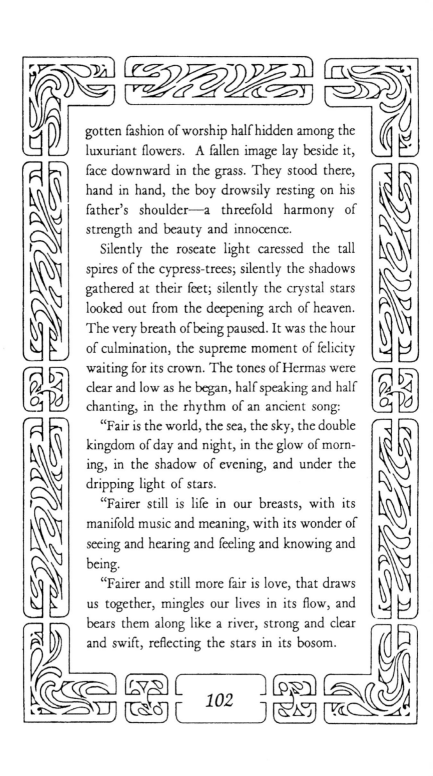

gotten fashion of worship half hidden among the luxuriant flowers. A fallen image lay beside it, face downward in the grass. They stood there, hand in hand, the boy drowsily resting on his father's shoulder—a threefold harmony of strength and beauty and innocence.

Silently the roseate light caressed the tall spires of the cypress-trees; silently the shadows gathered at their feet; silently the crystal stars looked out from the deepening arch of heaven. The very breath of being paused. It was the hour of culmination, the supreme moment of felicity waiting for its crown. The tones of Hermas were clear and low as he began, half speaking and half chanting, in the rhythm of an ancient song:

"Fair is the world, the sea, the sky, the double kingdom of day and night, in the glow of morning, in the shadow of evening, and under the dripping light of stars.

"Fairer still is life in our breasts, with its manifold music and meaning, with its wonder of seeing and hearing and feeling and knowing and being.

"Fairer and still more fair is love, that draws us together, mingles our lives in its flow, and bears them along like a river, strong and clear and swift, reflecting the stars in its bosom.

"Wide is our world; we are rich; we have all things. Life is abundant within us—a measureless deep. Deepest of all is our love, and it longs to speak.

"Come, thou final word! Come, thou crown of speech! Come, thou charm of peace! Open the gates of our hearts. Lift the weight of our joy and bear it upward.

"For all good gifts, for all perfect gifts, for love, for life, for the world, we praise, we bless, we thank—"

As a soaring bird, struck by an arrow, falls headlong from the sky, so the song of Hermas fell. At the end of his flight of gratitude there was nothing—a blank, a hollow space.

He looked for a face, and saw a void. He sought for a hand, and clasped vacancy. His heart was throbbing and swelling with passion; the bell swung to and fro within him, beating from side to side as if it would burst; but not a single note came from it. All the fulness of his feeling, that had risen upward like a living fountain, fell back from the empty sky, as cold as snow, as hard as hail, frozen and dead. There was no meaning in his happiness. No one had sent it to him. There was no one to thank for it. His felicity was a closed circle, a wall of eternal ice.

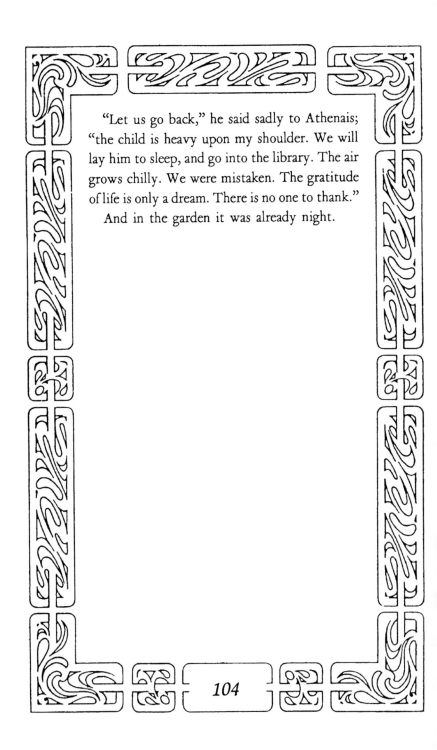

"Let us go back," he said sadly to Athenais; "the child is heavy upon my shoulder. We will lay him to sleep, and go into the library. The air grows chilly. We were mistaken. The gratitude of life is only a dream. There is no one to thank."

And in the garden it was already night.

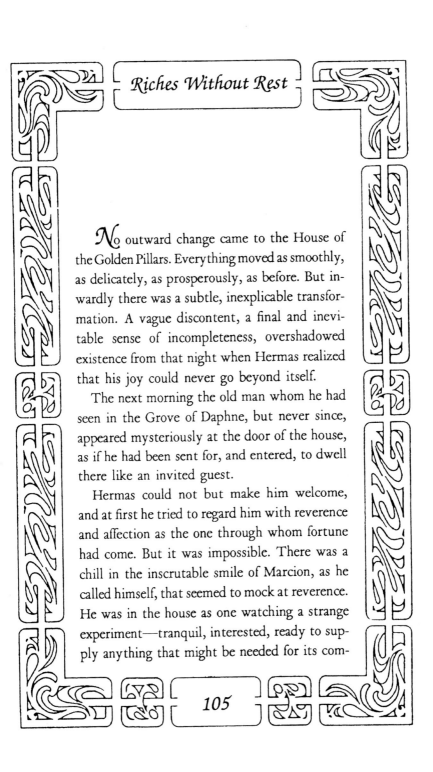

*N*o outward change came to the House of the Golden Pillars. Everything moved as smoothly, as delicately, as prosperously, as before. But inwardly there was a subtle, inexplicable transformation. A vague discontent, a final and inevitable sense of incompleteness, overshadowed existence from that night when Hermas realized that his joy could never go beyond itself.

The next morning the old man whom he had seen in the Grove of Daphne, but never since, appeared mysteriously at the door of the house, as if he had been sent for, and entered, to dwell there like an invited guest.

Hermas could not but make him welcome, and at first he tried to regard him with reverence and affection as the one through whom fortune had come. But it was impossible. There was a chill in the inscrutable smile of Marcion, as he called himself, that seemed to mock at reverence. He was in the house as one watching a strange experiment—tranquil, interested, ready to supply anything that might be needed for its completion, but thoroughly indifferent to the feelings of the subject; an anatomist of life, looking curiously to see how long it would continue, and how it would behave, after the heart had been removed.

In his presence Hermas was conscious of a certain irritation, a resentful anger against the calm, frigid scrutiny of the eyes that followed him everywhere, like a pair of spies, peering out over the smiling mouth and the long white beard.

"Why do you look at me so curiously?" asked Hermas, one morning, as they sat together in the library. "Do you see anything strange in me?"

"No," answered Marcion; "something familiar."

"And what is that?"

"A singular likeness to a discontented young man that I met some years ago in the Grove of Daphne."

"But why should that interest you? Surely it was to be expected."

"A thing that we expect often surprises us when we see it. Besides, my curiosity is piqued. I suspect you of keeping a secret from me."

"You are jesting with me. There is nothing in my life that you do not know. What is the secret?"

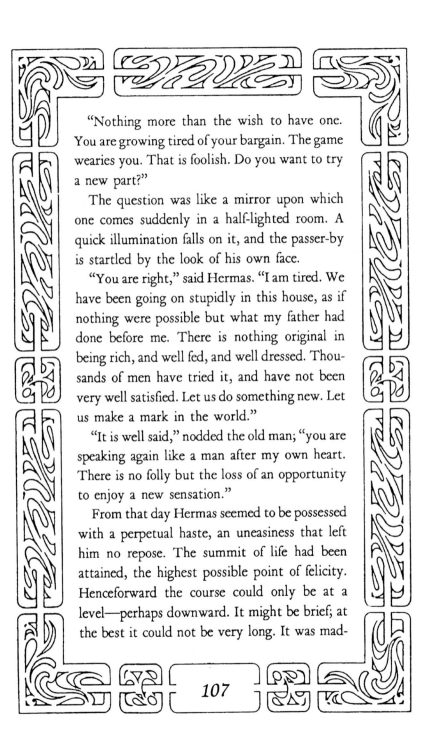

"Nothing more than the wish to have one. You are growing tired of your bargain. The game wearies you. That is foolish. Do you want to try a new part?"

The question was like a mirror upon which one comes suddenly in a half-lighted room. A quick illumination falls on it, and the passer-by is startled by the look of his own face.

"You are right," said Hermas. "I am tired. We have been going on stupidly in this house, as if nothing were possible but what my father had done before me. There is nothing original in being rich, and well fed, and well dressed. Thousands of men have tried it, and have not been very well satisfied. Let us do something new. Let us make a mark in the world."

"It is well said," nodded the old man; "you are speaking again like a man after my own heart. There is no folly but the loss of an opportunity to enjoy a new sensation."

From that day Hermas seemed to be possessed with a perpetual haste, an uneasiness that left him no repose. The summit of life had been attained, the highest possible point of felicity. Henceforward the course could only be at a level—perhaps downward. It might be brief; at the best it could not be very long. It was madness to lose a day, an hour. That would be the only fatal mistake: to forfeit anything of the bargain that he had made. He would have it, and hold it, and enjoy it all to the full. The world might have nothing better to give than it had already given; but surely it had many things that were new to bestow upon him, and Marcion should help him to find them.

Under his learned counsel the House of the Golden Pillars took on a new magnificence. Artists were brought from Corinth and Rome and Byzantium to adorn it with splendour. Its fame glittered around the world. Banquets of incredible luxury drew the most celebrated guests into its triclinium, and filled them with envious admiration. The bees swarmed and buzzed about the golden hive. The human insects, gorgeous moths of pleasure and greedy flies of appetite, parasites and flatterers and crowds of inquisitive idlers, danced and fluttered in the dazzling light that surrounded Hermas.

Everything that he touched prospered. He bought a tract of land in the Caucasus, and emeralds were discovered among the mountains. He sent a fleet of wheat-ships to Italy, and the price of grain doubled while it was on the way. He sought political favour with the emperor, and was rewarded with the governorship of the city. His name was a word to conjure with.

The beauty of Athenais lost nothing with the passing seasons, but grew more perfect, even under the inexplicable shade of dissatisfaction that sometimes veiled it as a translucent cloud that passes before the full moon. "Fair as the wife of Hermas" was a proverb in Antioch; and soon men began to add to it, "Beautiful as the son of Hermas"; for the child developed swiftly in that favouring clime. At nine years of age he was straight and strong, firm of limb and clear of eye. His brown head was on a level with his father's heart. He was the jewel of the House of the Golden Pillars; the pride of Hermas, the new Fortunatus.

That year another drop of success fell into his brimming cup. His black Numidian horses, which he had been training for three years for the world-renowned chariot-races of Antioch, won the victory over a score of rivals. Hermas received the prize carelessly from the judge's hands, and turned to drive once more around the circus, to show himself to the people. He lifted the eager boy into the chariot beside him to share his triumph. Here, indeed, was the glory of his life—this matchless son, his brighter

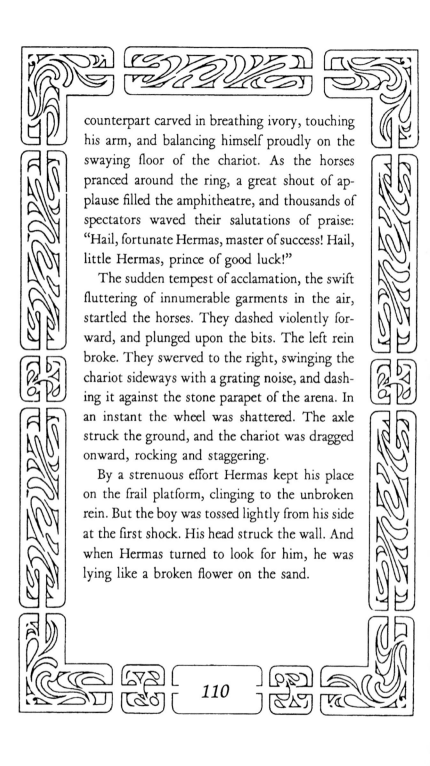

counterpart carved in breathing ivory, touching his arm, and balancing himself proudly on the swaying floor of the chariot. As the horses pranced around the ring, a great shout of applause filled the amphitheatre, and thousands of spectators waved their salutations of praise: "Hail, fortunate Hermas, master of success! Hail, little Hermas, prince of good luck!"

The sudden tempest of acclamation, the swift fluttering of innumerable garments in the air, startled the horses. They dashed violently forward, and plunged upon the bits. The left rein broke. They swerved to the right, swinging the chariot sideways with a grating noise, and dashing it against the stone parapet of the arena. In an instant the wheel was shattered. The axle struck the ground, and the chariot was dragged onward, rocking and staggering.

By a strenuous effort Hermas kept his place on the frail platform, clinging to the unbroken rein. But the boy was tossed lightly from his side at the first shock. His head struck the wall. And when Hermas turned to look for him, he was lying like a broken flower on the sand.

Great Fear
And Recovered Joy

They carried the boy in a litter to the House of the Golden Pillars, summoning the most skilful physician of Antioch to attend him. For hours the child was as quiet as death. Hermas watched the white eyelids, folded close like lily-buds at night, even as one watches for the morning. At last they opened; but the fire of fever was burning in the eyes, and the lips were moving in a wild delirium.

Hour after hour that sweet childish voice rang through the halls and chambers of the splendid, helpless house, now rising in shrill calls of distress and senseless laughter, now sinking in weariness and dull moaning. The stars waxed and waned; the sun rose and set; the roses bloomed and fell in the garden; the birds sang and slept among the jasmine-bowers. But in the heart of Hermas there was no song, no bloom, no light—only speechless anguish, and a certain fearful looking-for of desolation.

He was like a man in a nightmare. He saw the shapeless terror that was moving toward him, but he was impotent to stay or to escape it. He had done all that he could. There was nothing left but to wait.

He paced to and fro, now hurrying to the boy's bed as if he could not bear to be away from it, now turning back as if he could not endure to be near it. The people of the house, even Athenais, feared to speak to him, there was something so vacant and desperate in his face.

At nightfall, on the second of those eternal days, he shut himself in the library. The unfilled lamp had gone out, leaving a trail of smoke in the air. The sprigs of mignonette and rosemary, with which the room was sprinkled every day, were unrenewed, and scented the gloom with a close odor of decay. A costly manuscript of Theocritus was tumbled in disorder on the floor. Hermas sank into a chair like a man in whom the very spring of being is broken. Through the darkness some one drew near. He did not even lift his head. A hand touched him; a soft arm was laid over his shoulders. It was Athenais, kneeling beside him and speaking very low:

"Hermas—it is almost over—the child! His voice grows weaker hour by hour. He moans and calls for some one to help him; then he laughs. It breaks my heart. He has just fallen asleep. The

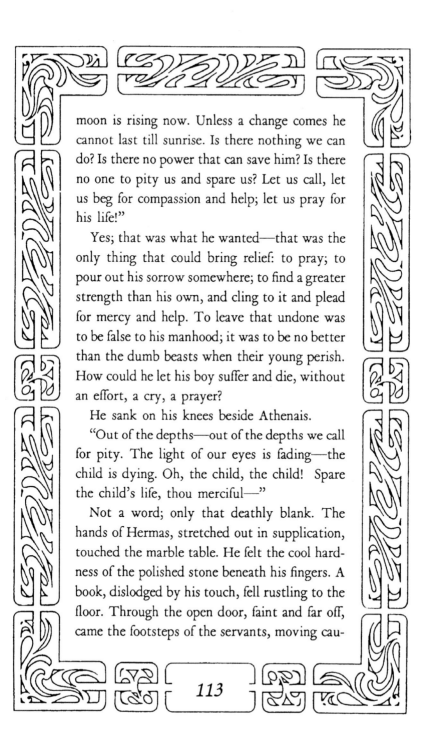

moon is rising now. Unless a change comes he cannot last till sunrise. Is there nothing we can do? Is there no power that can save him? Is there no one to pity us and spare us? Let us call, let us beg for compassion and help; let us pray for his life!"

Yes; that was what he wanted—that was the only thing that could bring relief: to pray; to pour out his sorrow somewhere; to find a greater strength than his own, and cling to it and plead for mercy and help. To leave that undone was to be false to his manhood; it was to be no better than the dumb beasts when their young perish. How could he let his boy suffer and die, without an effort, a cry, a prayer?

He sank on his knees beside Athenais.

"Out of the depths—out of the depths we call for pity. The light of our eyes is fading—the child is dying. Oh, the child, the child! Spare the child's life, thou merciful—"

Not a word; only that deathly blank. The hands of Hermas, stretched out in supplication, touched the marble table. He felt the cool hardness of the polished stone beneath his fingers. A book, dislodged by his touch, fell rustling to the floor. Through the open door, faint and far off, came the footsteps of the servants, moving cautiously. The heart of Hermas was like a lump of ice in his bosom. He rose slowly to his feet, lifting Athenais with him.

"It is in vain," he said; "there is nothing for us to do. Long ago I knew something. I think it would have helped us. But I have forgotten it. It is all gone. But I would give all that I have, if I could bring it back again now, at this hour, in this time of our bitter trouble."

A slave entered the room while he was speaking, and approached hesitatingly.

"Master," he said, "John of Antioch, whom we were forbidden to admit to the house, has come again. He would take no denial. Even now he waits in the peristyle; and the old man Marcion is with him, seeking to turn him away."

"Come," said Hermas to his wife, "let us go to him; for I think I see the beginning of a way that may lead us out of this dreadful darkness."

In the central hall the two men were standing; Marcion, with disdainful eyes and sneering lips, taunting the unbidden guest to depart; John silent, quiet, patient, while the wondering slaves looked on in dismay. He lifted his searching gaze to the haggard face of Hermas.

"My son, I knew that I should see you again, even though you did not send for me. I have

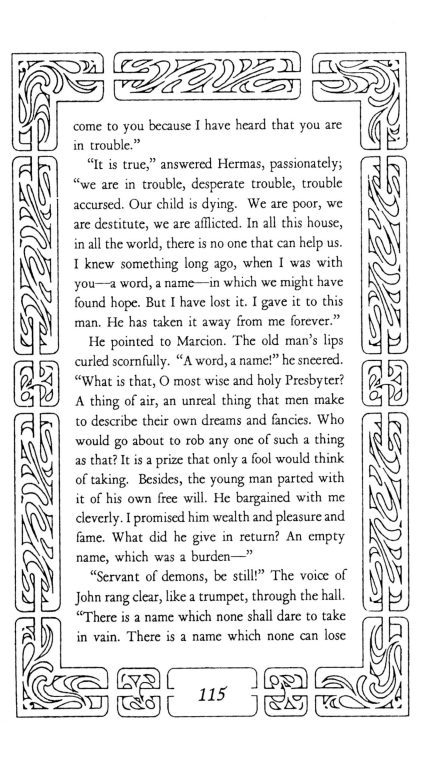

come to you because I have heard that you are in trouble."

"It is true," answered Hermas, passionately; "we are in trouble, desperate trouble, trouble accursed. Our child is dying. We are poor, we are destitute, we are afflicted. In all this house, in all the world, there is no one that can help us. I knew something long ago, when I was with you—a word, a name—in which we might have found hope. But I have lost it. I gave it to this man. He has taken it away from me forever."

He pointed to Marcion. The old man's lips curled scornfully. "A word, a name!" he sneered. "What is that, O most wise and holy Presbyter? A thing of air, an unreal thing that men make to describe their own dreams and fancies. Who would go about to rob any one of such a thing as that? It is a prize that only a fool would think of taking. Besides, the young man parted with it of his own free will. He bargained with me cleverly. I promised him wealth and pleasure and fame. What did he give in return? An empty name, which was a burden—"

"Servant of demons, be still!" The voice of John rang clear, like a trumpet, through the hall. "There is a name which none shall dare to take in vain. There is a name which none can lose without being lost. There is a name at which the devils tremble. Depart quickly, before I speak it!"

Marcion had shrunk into the shadow of one of the pillars. A bright lamp near him tottered on its pedestal and fell with a crash. In the confusion he vanished, as noiselessly as a shade.

John turned to Hermas, and his tone softened as he said:

"My son, you have sinned deeper than you know. The word with which you parted so lightly is the keyword of all life and joy and peace. Without it the world has no meaning, and existence no rest, and death no refuge. It is the word that purifies love, and comforts grief, and keeps hope alive forever. It is the most precious thing that ever ear has heard, or mind has known, or heart has conceived. It is the name of Him who has given us life and breath and all things richly to enjoy; the name of Him who, though we may forget Him, never forgets us; the name of Him who pities us as you pity your suffering child; the name of Him who, though we wander far from Him, seeks us in the wilderness, and sent His Son, even as His Son has sent me this night, to breathe again that forgotten name in the heart that is perishing without it.

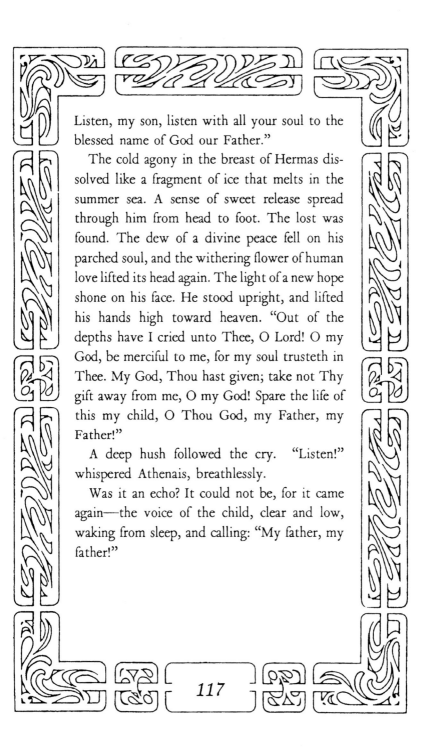

Listen, my son, listen with all your soul to the blessed name of God our Father."

The cold agony in the breast of Hermas dissolved like a fragment of ice that melts in the summer sea. A sense of sweet release spread through him from head to foot. The lost was found. The dew of a divine peace fell on his parched soul, and the withering flower of human love lifted its head again. The light of a new hope shone on his face. He stood upright, and lifted his hands high toward heaven. "Out of the depths have I cried unto Thee, O Lord! O my God, be merciful to me, for my soul trusteth in Thee. My God, Thou hast given; take not Thy gift away from me, O my God! Spare the life of this my child, O Thou God, my Father, my Father!"

A deep hush followed the cry. "Listen!" whispered Athenais, breathlessly.

Was it an echo? It could not be, for it came again—the voice of the child, clear and low, waking from sleep, and calling: "My father, my father!"

The Spirit
of Christmas

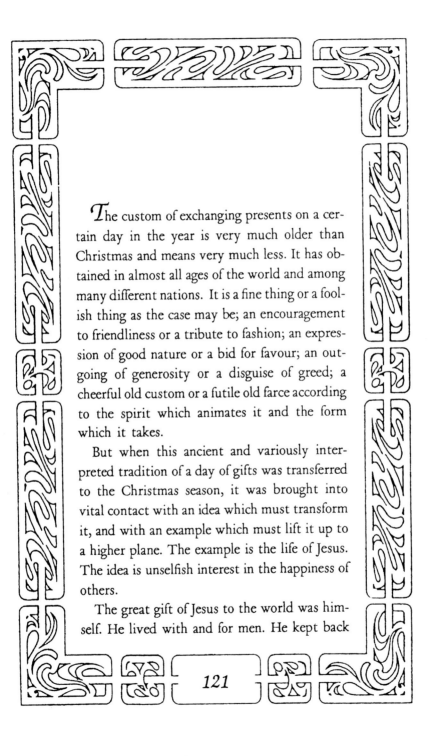

The custom of exchanging presents on a certain day in the year is very much older than Christmas and means very much less. It has obtained in almost all ages of the world and among many different nations. It is a fine thing or a foolish thing as the case may be; an encouragement to friendliness or a tribute to fashion; an expression of good nature or a bid for favour; an outgoing of generosity or a disguise of greed; a cheerful old custom or a futile old farce according to the spirit which animates it and the form which it takes.

But when this ancient and variously interpreted tradition of a day of gifts was transferred to the Christmas season, it was brought into vital contact with an idea which must transform it, and with an example which must lift it up to a higher plane. The example is the life of Jesus. The idea is unselfish interest in the happiness of others.

The great gift of Jesus to the world was himself. He lived with and for men. He kept back

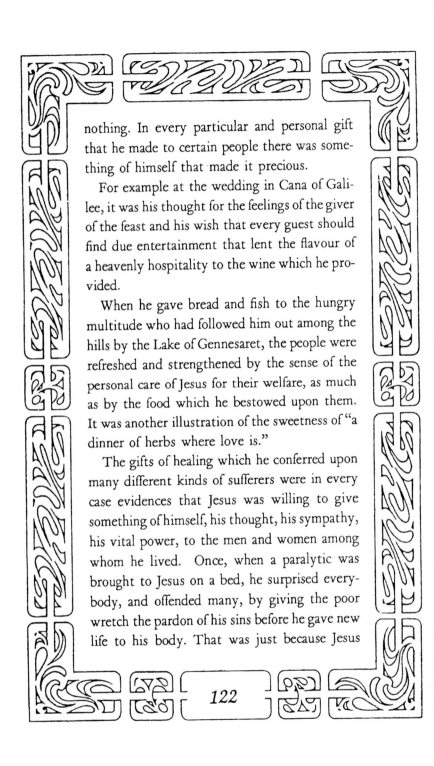

nothing. In every particular and personal gift that he made to certain people there was something of himself that made it precious.

For example at the wedding in Cana of Galilee, it was his thought for the feelings of the giver of the feast and his wish that every guest should find due entertainment that lent the flavour of a heavenly hospitality to the wine which he provided.

When he gave bread and fish to the hungry multitude who had followed him out among the hills by the Lake of Gennesaret, the people were refreshed and strengthened by the sense of the personal care of Jesus for their welfare, as much as by the food which he bestowed upon them. It was another illustration of the sweetness of "a dinner of herbs where love is."

The gifts of healing which he conferred upon many different kinds of sufferers were in every case evidences that Jesus was willing to give something of himself, his thought, his sympathy, his vital power, to the men and women among whom he lived. Once, when a paralytic was brought to Jesus on a bed, he surprised everybody, and offended many, by giving the poor wretch the pardon of his sins before he gave new life to his body. That was just because Jesus thought before he gave; because he desired to satisfy the deepest need; because in fact he gave something of himself in every gift. All true Christmas-giving ought to be after this pattern.

Not that it must all be solemn and serious. For the most part it deals with little wants, little joys, little tokens of friendly feeling. But the feeling must be more than the token; else the gift does not really belong to Christmas.

It takes time and effort and unselfish expenditure of strength to make gifts in this way. But it is the only way that fits the season.

The finest Christmas gift is not the one that costs the most money but the one that carries the most love.

But how seldom Christmas comes——only once a year; and how soon it is over——a night and a day! If that is the whole of it, it seems not much more durable than the little toys that one buys of a fakir on the street-corner. They run for an hour and then the spring breaks and the legs come off and nothing remains but a contribution to the dust heap.

But surely that need not and ought not to be

the whole of Christmas—only a single day of generosity ransomed from the dull servitude of a selfish year—only a single night of merry-making celebrated in the slave-quarters of a selfish race! If every gift is the token of a personal thought, a friendly feeling, an unselfish interest in the joy of others, then the thought, the feeling, the interest may remain after the gift is made.

The little present or the rare and long-wished-for gift (it matters not whether the vessel be of gold, or silver, or iron, or wood, or clay, or just a small bit of birch bark folded into a cup) may carry a message something like this:

"I am thinking of you today, because it is Christmas and I wish you happiness. And tomorrow, because it will be the day after Christmas, I shall still wish you happiness; and so on, clear through the year. I may not be able to tell you about it every day because I may be far away; or because both of us may be very busy; or perhaps because I cannot even afford to pay the postage on so many letters or find the time to write them. But that makes no difference. The thought and the wish will be here just the same. In my work and in the business of life, I mean to try not to be unfair to you or injure you in any way. In my pleasure, if we can be together I would like to share the fun with you. Whatever joy or success comes to you will make me glad. Without pretense and in plain words, goodwill to you is what I mean, in the Spirit of Christmas."

It is not necessary to put a message like this into high-flown language, to swear absolute devotion and deathless consecration. In love and friendship, small, steady payments on a gold basis are better than immense promissory notes. Nor, indeed, is it always necessary to put the message into words at all, nor even to convey it by a tangible token. To feel it and to act it out— that is the main thing.

There are a great many people in the world whom we know more or less, but to whom for various reasons we cannot very well send a Christmas gift. But there is hardly one in all the circles of our acquaintance with whom we may not exchange the touch of Christmas life.

In the outer circles, cheerful greetings, courtesy, consideration; in the inner circles, sympathetic interest, hearty congratulations, honest encouragement; in the inmost circle, comradeship, helpfulness, tenderness—

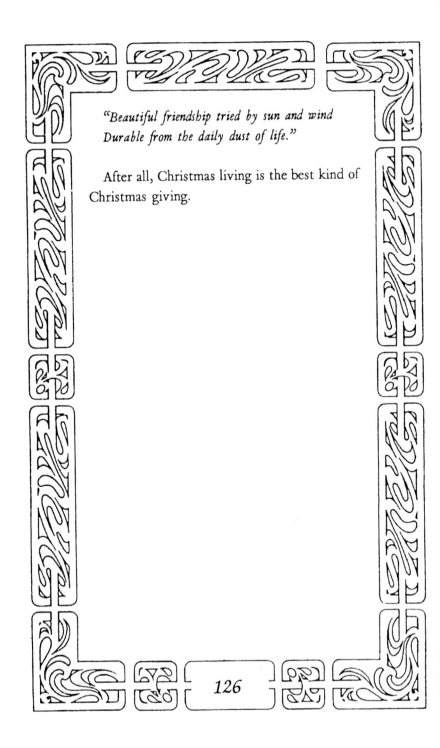

"Beautiful friendship tried by sun and wind
Durable from the daily dust of life."

After all, Christmas living is the best kind of Christmas giving.

THE STORY
OF THE OTHER WISE MAN

OTHER FINE ENTHEA TITLES

The Tao of Meow
A Cat's Guide to Self-Gratification
by Waldo Japussy
$17.50

The Story of God
by Carl Japikse
$18.99

Fear No Evil
by Robert Leichtman, M.D.
$9.95

Working with Angels
by Robert Leichtman, M.D. & Carl Japikse
$7.95

Enjoying Poetry
by Carl Japikse
$12.95

A Deodorizer of Dead Dogs
tall tales by Ambrose Bierce
$15.99